The Timeless Tales
of
Reginald Bretnor

selected and edited by
Fred Flaxman
with an introduction by
Poul Anderson

STORY BOOKS
Publishers

©1997 by Story Books, Publishers. All rights reserved.

Printed in the United States of America.

No part of this book may be reproduced or transmitted in any form or by any means, electronic or mechanical, including photocopying, recording, or by any information storage and retrieval system, without the written permission of the publisher, except by a reviewer quoting brief passages in a magazine, newspaper, or electronic medium. Address inquiries to the publisher.

Cover illustration by Reginald Bretnor. Cover and book design by Fred Flaxman. Proofreading by Annick Story Flaxman, Tana Jencks and Ken Droscher.

This first edition is limited to 1,000 hand-numbered books, of which this is number _____, plus review copies. Additional copies are available from the publisher. To order, send $12.95 plus $3 mailing/packaging per book to:

Story Books

Story Lane, 385 Hawk Road
Medford, Oregon 97501-8518

Telephone: (541) 772-7305
Fax: (541) 779-7176
E-Mail: fflaxman@jeffnet.org

ISBN 1-891513-00-1

*In Memory of Reginald Bretnor
with thanks for providing the world
with these delightful stories*

Contents

1. Cat 12
A professor learns to understand and speak Cat — the language. Or is he faking it and fooling everyone?

2. Maybe Just a Little One 34
A high school physics teacher learns how to get nuclear power from Mexican beans, but his discovery is not exactly appreciated by the outside world!

3. Unknown Things 53
An antique collector will pay virtually any price for items he can't figure out.

4. Bug-Getter 65
A starving artist, living in terrible conditions, has to fight with collection agencies, landlords, and an invasion of crickets which are destroying his paintings.

5. Aunt's Flight 70
Charles Lindbergh was the first man to fly alone across the Atlantic — but he was not the first *person* to do so.

6. Dr. Birdmouse 85
Dr. Vandercook, from Earth, lands on the planet Eetwee, where it turns out each inhabitant is a curious blend of species. Vandercook knows he has it made on Earth if he can bring a few of these creatures back on his spaceship. But that's not so easy to do.

7. Man on Top 105
Geoffrey Barbank may have given the world the impression that he was the first man to reach the summit of Mt. Everest, but his conscience and his climbing partner know better.

8. Beasts that Perish 113
There is an epidemic of fatal, one-car crashes. A top-secret government team is assigned to find out why.

Contents

9. Without (General) Issue 137
Why the Commander-in-Chief absolutely refuses to permit women officers as members of Space Force First Contact teams.

10. Mating Season 145
In a California boarding house, the tenants find out that two of the boarders are to be married. The tall and skinny looks of the couple results in a running joke about the young woman being a praying mantis and the young man her mate. The joke gets out of hand.

11. Mrs. Pigafetta Swims Well 160
Pietro, a famous and handsome Italian opera singer, is rescued by Mrs. Pigafetta following a storm at sea. Love blossoms between them until she brings up the subject of marriage. Pietro then awakes to the fact that she's half fish and does not sing too well!

12. The Murderers' Circle 170
Why is the murder rate so low in England compared to the United States? The startling truth is revealed.

13. Paper Tiger 180
The differences between the United States and China are finally resolved as the result of a unique meeting of their top leaders.

14. Fungo the Unrighteous 199
Can King Fungo and his beloved Clysomel reign over their prosperous and happy three kingdoms, despite the dreadful predictions of the royal astrologer?

15. All the Tea in China 211
A young man learns how the Devil punished his great uncle for his greed and mean spirit.

About the Author

Reginald Bretnor (1911-1992) was born Alfred Reginald Kahn in Vladivostok, Siberia. He was the son of a Latvian Jewish banker and an English governess. The family moved to Japan in 1917, then to San Diego, California, in 1920. Bretnor, whose name was taken from the maiden name of his maternal grandmother and who many acquaintances thought to be the perfect English gentleman, never left the United States in the 72 years he lived here and did not once set foot in Great Britain.

Bretnor wrote fantasy, science fiction, mysteries, children's stories, military theory and public affairs articles. For half a century he also wrote stories and articles about cats, and was credited as the translator for the first book that we know of ever published on the subject: Moncrif's *Les Chats* (1727).

Bretnor wrote with a good sense of humor and was fascinated by puns. Under the pseudonym of Grendel Briarton, he authored *Through Time and Space with Ferdinand Feghoot*, a series of shaggy-dog-story-like science fiction puns which ran for years in *Fantasy & Science Fiction, Venture* and *Isaac Asimov's Science Fiction* magazines. Paradox Press published a paperback *Feghoot* collection in 1962. The Mirage Press published two more recent editions: *The Compleat Feghoot* and *The (Even More) Compleat Feghoot*.

Bretnor penned a mystery novel, *A Killing in Swords*, published by Pocket Books in 1978. A science fiction novella, *Gilpin's Space*, which appeared as the lead story in *Fantasy & Science Fiction* magazine, was later expanded into a full novel. His most recent novel was *Schimmelhorn's Gold*. A collection of Bretnor's stories

About the Author

about an oversexed octogenarian idiot/genius, *The Schimmelhorn File*, was published by Ace Books.

Bretnor's first science fiction story, "Maybe Just a Little One," appeared in *Harper's Magazine* in August, 1947. After that his fiction was published in all the major science fiction magazines and in *Esquire, Today's Woman, Southwest Review, Ellery Queen's Mystery Magazine, Alfred Hitchcock Magazine* and many other publications.

As a science fiction writer, editor and authority, Bretnor was interested in known and unexplained phenomena, and writings on the subject filled three of the books he edited: *The Craft of Science Fiction* (Harper & Row, 1976), *Science Fiction, Today and Tomorrow* (Harper & Row, 1974) and a three-volume anthology, *The Future at War* (Ace Books). *Science Fiction, Today and Tomorrow* was also published as a Penguin paperback. *The Craft of Science Fiction* was published as a paperback by Barnes & Noble. These books contain chapters by Asimov, Clarke, Boucher, Herbert, Pohl, Clement, Ellison, Anderson and many other leading science fiction writers, including Bretnor himself. Bretnor was the author of the article on science fiction in two editions of the *Encyclopedia Britannica*.

About the Editor

Fred Flaxman is an award-winning writer, columnist, television producer and radio commentator. He is the owner of the Bretnor Literary Estate and Archives.

His books-in-progress include *Sixty Slices of Life... on Wry* and *Doctors, Dentists, Dishwashers & Other Demons of Modern Life*. He writes a monthly *Compact Discoveries* column for print and Internet distribution. His World Wide Web site is http://www.jeffnet.org/fflaxman.

Introduction

Memorials are for the living.

This book is a tribute to the late Reginald Bretnor, but those who have gathered together here a part of his work give themselves a gift — an enduring pleasure in these delightful short stories. More importantly, they give them to the world. People who never knew Bretnor personally or who have known little of what he did will find some wonderful reading. They too will feel his spirit: genial, vivacious, widely informed, deeply concerned. May this go on for many generations to come.

That will serve a cause he cherished. It was not that he demanded fame for himself. What he fought for was a restoration of public literacy, the survival in our civilization of art and thought — honest art, clear thought, rather than the fashionable frauds he disdained. The fact is, however, that his contributions to the heritage are not minor.

No doubt this assertion will surprise those whose acquaintance with his writing is superficial or nil. They may recall him as the originator of the "Feghoot," a kind of short-short story leading with inexorable logic to an outrageous pun. They may remember the saga of Papa Schimmelhorn, its gusto and merriment. Too often, that is all that will come to mind.

Introduction

Taken simply by itself, it is not so little. Has mirth no value? Are the comedy of Aristophanes and Molière, the wit of Chesterton and Knox, yes, the farce of Wodehouse, negligible? Humor successfully brought off is a high and rare accomplishment.

Yet it was by no means Reginald Bretnor's only accomplishment, nor his most significant.

He was a master of the short story in general. There never have been many. If it is to be done right, it requires very special skills. True, mediocre short stories are legion. Likewise are mediocre sonnets. But, to take a nearly random example, with its concentration, its lapidary *structure*, Shakespeare's 32nd ("If thou survive my well-contented day...") evokes an artist who is also a lover and strikes directly into his innermost being. Now add up just how much Bretnor's *Unknown Things* manages to say in its few pages about collectors and their curious world, sexuality, and passionless cruelty. No novel can have such a cold impact: not of the sword but of the poignard.

He could do a novel when he chose, with comparable style, inventiveness, and narrative pace. It is our misfortune that he seldom did.

As for the material of his fiction, it includes everyday life, made luminous, and crime, ingeniously devised, in contemporary settings. Most of it, though, is science fiction or fantasy. Long before these fields attained widespread popularity and a measure of academic respectability, he was proud to work in them and to claim for them equality with every other form. In making good that claim, he played a leading part.

Besides his stories, this was through his critical efforts, the essays and the three symposium books he conceived and edited. He might have tut-tutted at my adjective, since the pretentious twaddle that usually passes for criticism was an object of his derision, but I mean it in the sense of "examining profoundly and sympathetically." He pioneered, raising landmarks for those who came after.

Military matters engaged him equally. He neither glorified war nor went into hysterical denunciations of it. He studied it, considered how means might be kept proportionate to ends, published thought-provoking suggestions, and invented a field weapon, which, ignored at the time, was later independently duplicated and taken into use.

I forget who it was who said every fine writer owes his or her country a translation, but Bretnor paid the debt from the French of Moncrif's charming eighteenth-century *Cats*. Altogether, his range of interests and knowledge was vast, as the stories amply demonstrate.

His life was similarly diversified. He was born in 1911 in Vladivostok, to a Russian father and English mother. The family presently moved to Japan and thence to the United States, of which he became a citizen in 1934. Among the numerous jobs he held during the Depression was a stint as a soldier in the last horse cavalry the Army ever maintained. Medically discharged, he served in the Japanese section of our Office of War Information, absorbed after the end of hostilities by the State Department.

In 1947 he resigned to write full time and settled in Berkeley, California. There he married Helen Harding, a librarian at the University of California and herself a writer and translator. She was a dear person; everyone who knew her mourned when she died in 1967. Two

Introduction

years afterward, Reg married his colleague Rosalie Leveille. She too was lovable, but it did not become my privilege to know her well, because they went to live in Oregon, first Jacksonville, then Medford. She died in 1988. He worked quietly and uncomplainingly on until his own peaceful death in 1992.

In person he was a big, hearty man with somewhat of a British accent. His conversation, like his writing, sparkled with humor but could get wholly serious. He raised cats, cooked gourmet meals, and was a born collector, the sort who understands his material — which, in his case, ranged from Japanese swords to firearms and, always, books.

His politics was conservative, not reactionary but respectful of ancient traditions and basic decencies. Strongly held, none of his opinions on various subjects lessened his warmth for friends who disagreed. During his time in California he met monthly with Anthony Boucher, my wife, myself, and a few others for poker. Households took turns hosting these games, and an amicable rivalry developed as to who could set forth the best dinner; though play was fierce, the stakes were small and the purpose, really, fellowship. Those years are long ended, but the laughter echoes in me still. All Reg's vividness does.

Come into this book and share.

— Poul Anderson

Poul Anderson's many science fiction novels have been published by St. Martin's Press, Tor, Ace, Berkley Books, Doubleday and Avalon. They include War of the Gods *(1997),* Fleet of Stars *(1997),* Harvest the Fire *(1995),* Harvest of Stars *(1993),* The Time Patrol *(1991), and* The Shield of Time *(1990). His short stories have been published in all the leading science fiction magazines and in several collections.*

1
Cat

This story was first published in The Magazine of Fantasy & Science Fiction *in April, 1953, and may also have appeared in foreign editions of this magazine. It was reprinted in Australia, France and Spain and was included in the book* The Eureka Years: Boucher and McComas's Magazine of Fantasy and Science Fiction, 1949-1954, *published by Bantam Books in 1982.*

I had no premonition of disaster when Smithby married Cynthia Carmichael and took her off on his sabbatical. No inner voice whispered its awful warning in my ear when it was rumored that he was spending his year of leave in research of a strangely private nature. Even as his department head, how could I know that he was bringing *Cat* into the world?

His year drew to a close, my own sabbatical began, and off I went — intending, after three therapeutic months in sunny Italy, to seek the scholarly seclusion of Scotland's National Library for the remainder of my time. But it was not to be. Scarcely a week after I arrived in Edinburgh, the letter came.

Did I say "letter"? There was no letter in the grimy envelope which had followed my wandering path from Naples north. It contained only a brief note and an enormous clipping from some cheap green newspaper.

I glanced at the curt message:

Cat

Dear Christopher,
Smithby has betrayed our tradition and our trust. Your entire department is in turmoil. Three of us have already tendered our resignations.

Witherspoon

For one dreadful moment, I closed my eyes; and Smithby's face, a pallid mask of modest erudition, appeared before me. Then, with trembling fingers, I opened up the clipping:

WIFE'S LOVE PROMPTS SCIENCE TRIUMPH!
Young Bogwood Prof Wins Plaudits
For First Cat Language Studies!

the headlines screamed with a malicious glee, above a photograph of Smithby and his spouse, each grasping a large feline. Stupefied, I read on:

> New Haven, August 5: For the first time in nearly a century Bogwood College flashed into the limelight today as Emerson Smithby, professor of English Literature, bared what scientists acclaim as the outstanding discovery of the age — the language spoken by cats.
>
> Giving full credit to his wife, blonde curvaceous Cynthia Smithby, the surprisingly youthful savant this morning outlined highlights of the gruelling research that enabled him to break down the hitherto insurmountable barrier between man and the so-called lower animals.
>
> Professor Smithby said, in part:
> "Cats not only have a language —they have a complex culture not basically dissimilar to our own. I first began to suspect this when Mrs. Smithby and I were honeymooning; and she assisted me untiringly, lending both her own cats for the enquiry.
>
> "As soon as we convinced them of the importance of the project, we progressed rapidly. In less than two months, we were able to prattle conversational *Cat* with some fluency."

The Timeless Tales of Reginald Bretnor

> Professor Smithby then revealed that he has already issued a text for beginners: *Cat, Its Basic Grammar, Pronunciation, and General Usage.*
>
> He refused, however, to discuss a rumor that, through the efforts of Gregory Morton, widely known cat fancier and member of Bogwood's Board of Regents, courses in *Cat* will shortly be added to the curriculum.
>
> Professor Christopher Flewkes, head of Dr. Smithby's department, could not be reached for comment.

I sat there staring. Lucid thought was impossible. Blind instinct told me that Bogwood was in peril — that Bogwood needed me — that I must catch the first boat back.

Nothing could have prepared me for the reception Fate had arranged in the Faculty Club on the night of my return. Perhaps the bright light over the desk in the lobby blinded me as I entered; perhaps my preoccupation with my own harried thoughts prevented me from seeing the cat. Whatever the reason, I had no inkling of its presence until its sudden scream informed the world that I had stepped upon its tail.

It was a strange tableau. The cat had fled, leaving me standing beside my fallen bag in the middle of the floor. From behind the desk, the clerk — a young Oriental hired in my absence — glared at me through a pair of those curious spectacles known, I believe, as harlequins.

"Do you, my sir," he demanded with placid insolence, "practice to come and step upon the guests? If so, go to where you belong."

I stifled my anger. "See here," I replied, "I am Dr. Flewkes — Christopher Flewkes."

The fellow smiled. "Then stepping will be an accident. I have knowledge of you. You are Flewkes. I am Yu."

Cat

I thought: *The man, of course, is mad!* "Indeed? "I exclaimed. "You are me?"

Still smiling, he shook his head gravely. "It is not Mee. It is Yu — Beowulf Yu. I have named myself after an English literature. You will be glad."

"Very well," I snapped, "you are Yu. Is my room ready?"

Yu bowed, unruffled. "I am here for studying, "he informed me. "At the night, I am a clerk; at the day, I am studying *Cat* with some progress. In *Cat*, I am even possible to get a passing grade."

"Is my room ready?" I repeated grimly.

"In a certainty, my sir," said Yu. "At the moment, I will accompany with my presence. Now I must assure our guest of your apologies — "

He went to the cat where it sat nursing its bruised appendage in a corner. *"Ee-owr-r,"* he said, very courteously. *"Meow, meeiu mr-r-ou."*

The cat paid no attention whatsoever; and Yu, with a worried frown, hastily took a small volume from his pocket, referred to it, and repeated his original comment several times.

Finally, the animal raised its head. "Meow," it said plaintively.

Yu bowed. Then he turned to me happily. "You are forgiven, for it is a cultured one. Now we ascend upstairs."

I nodded feebly. As we turned toward the staircase, I saw that the lobby was full of cats. They were on the chairs, on the rugs, before the fire. They were even on the mantel under the portrait of Ebenezer Bogwood.

I entered my room. In a daze, I heard Yu's ungrammatical goodnight at my door. Wearily I sat down on the bed — and, in doing so, I spied the *Announcement of Courses* for the current semester lying on the bedside table. I fought against the urge to pick it up — but I was powerless. I reached for it, opened it, turned the pages. And I saw:

Department of Feline Languages
Emerson Smithby, Ph.D., Chairman

This was followed by a list of courses — *Cat* 100A (Elementary), *Cat* 212 (Philology), *Cat* 227 (Literature) — and by other pertinent data, including the information that all instruction was in the hands of Mr. and Mrs. Smithby.

Hopelessly, until day was breaking, I wept for Bogwood.

I did not wake until shortly before the luncheon hour, when the telephone rang to tell me that Witherspoon was awaiting me downstairs; and sad indeed were my thoughts as I forced myself to rise and dress. Witherspoon's note had mentioned resignation from the faculty; and now the impulse came to me that perhaps I should join him in his tragic withdrawal from the academic world, that perhaps we both had been outmoded by the science of a newer age. Finally, with clothing draggled and beard uncombed, I stumbled down the stairs.

I entered the lobby, and heard that familiar voice greeting me, and saw those long shapeless tweeds unfolding from a chair by the fireplace.

"Bertrand!" I cried out, and in a moment I had him by the hand.

I gaped at him in my astonishment. Was this the gentle, melancholy Witherspoon whom I had known?

Cat

He still stooped; his gray locks were as sparse as they had ever been. But I saw instantly that the old Witherspoon had vanished — that here was a man of iron!

He seemed to read my mind. Leading me to a chair, he brushed a cat aside so that I might sit there. "Christopher," he said, his high voice very firm, "I am still at my post. The time has come to fight — and fight we shall!"

At this, my heart filled with black despair for our lost cause. "How can we fight, Bertrand?" I exclaimed, pointing at the feline population of the room.

Witherspoon seated himself beside me. "Have courage, Christopher! These wretched creatures," he gestured at the cats, "are not to blame. Even Morton, vile as he is, is but a tool. Our enemy is Smithby. We must destroy him by fair means or foul!"

His eyes almost flashed as he said it. He lowered his voice to a conspiratorial whisper. "I've planned the strategy of our campaign," he hissed. "Shall I reveal it to you?"

"Do, by all means," said I, leaning forward eagerly.

But Witherspoon had no chance to answer me. Even as I spoke, his glance shifted. Fists clenched, narrow brow frowning sheer hatred, he glared past me at the lobby's entrance.

I had not noticed those who passed through to the dining room during our conversation. But now I looked about me — and beheld, coming across the floor, Smithby and Cynthia Smithby, with Beowulf Yu trailing in their wake. A long black cat was draped over Mrs. Smithby's shoulders in startling contrast to the coiled golden hair above it. Another cat, a Siamese, was carrying on a pleasant tête-à-tête with Smithby, who bore it in his arms.

I heard Witherspoon gnash his teeth in my ear. "Look at her!" he muttered viciously. "She looks like a cross between a cream puff and a Valkyrie."

The description, I must say, surprised me — later I learned that Witherspoon had heard it from a student. Still, it was not inaccurate. But for her heroic stature — dwarfing her husband by half a dozen inches — Cynthia Smithby would have suited Charles II to a T. She resembled Herrick's Julia: a splendid figure rather too ample for the modern fashion, a small red mouth, a tiny rounded chin, a rolling eye.

She was the first to see me. Instantly, an elfin smile touched her lips, and she changed her course. Head high, she came toward me.

I drew myself erect, to await her with a stern and uncompromising countenance. I knew that Witherspoon was wrong. Here was our enemy! Here was the Lilith who had seduced a weakling from the stony path of sober scholarship! I knew at once that there must be no pretense, that I must make my attitude quite clear.

Flushed and radiant, up she came. "Dear Dr. Flewkes!" said she, her voice low and musical. "What a delightful surprise! I am most glad to find you once again among us." She lowered her lashes in mock modesty. "And so is Emerson. Are you not, Emerson?"

Smithby blushed with embarrassment, fidgeted with a thin book he was carrying, and nodded with obvious pleasure.

"So much has happened since you went away," she went on, "so much that is very wonderful. But then —"

Cat

She laughed a pretty laugh. "You can catch up by attending Emerson's seminars."

I forced myself to look into her eyes. "Madam," I declared coldly, "half my life has been devoted to the service of this institution and to the preservation of its austere ideals. I can only hang my head in shame when I observe the sad decay of what was once a great tradition. Neither by word nor deed will I condone this treachery!"

Out of the corner of my eye, I saw a hurt look come over Smithby's face; I saw Beowulf Yu gape stupidly. For an instant, too, Cynthia Smithby pouted like some sensitive child suddenly rebuked. Then, with a toss of her head, "Mr. Flewkes," she said, "truly I am glad that you take this stand, for here — " she turned to Smithby, "here is the challenge that we need. Your genius, Emerson, will surmount this wall of classical conservatism. Our present project is certain to succeed. Then we will have proof positive and undeniable, and Dr. Flewkes will come to you with his apologies."

"Oh, not to me — " There was a calf-like worship in Smithby's eyes. "To you, Cynthia dear. The credit will be yours. The world will know that you have done it all!"

Beowulf giggled. "Then Flewkes will also make research in *Cat*." He peered at me through his harlequins. "I can give help. *Cat* words have one nice syllable, like Cantonese."

"Why, Beowulf — " Cynthia Smithby smiled archly. "You must devote your time to learning it yourself. You've failed every other course, you know. But let's have luncheon. Come." She took Smithby's arm. "And now, dear Dr. Flewkes, we bid you — *miaow*."

The Timeless Tales of Reginald Bretnor

As the dining room door closed behind them, I slumped back heavily into my chair. "My God, Bertrand," I muttered, "she — she *mewed* at me!"

"I believe," he answered, "that she was saying good-bye to you in *Cat*."

I wiped an icy perspiration from my forehead. "It is not Smithby who is the evil genius — it is she!"

"Nonsense!" snapped Witherspoon. "It's simply that she wears no brassiere — and you are too impressionable."

I flushed. "But — but what of her new project?"

"All froth and foolishness, believe me. Some silly toy her husband's given her. How could it be more? She does not even have her Ph. D."

This argument, of course, was quite unanswerable. I held my peace.

"He is the culprit," continued Witherspoon. "Surely you saw that small book he was carrying? It is his latest work — *Back Fence Ballads, Translated from the Original Cat*. He sings them, Christopher, to all his students, accompanying himself upon the lute. I have been told that his caterwauling is magnificent. And there's the extension course for lion tamers, conducted in the evenings. It has brought strange folk to Bogwood, I assure you."

He broke off. He pointed an apocalyptic finger to the heavens. "Do you wonder," he cried, "that I have taken desperate measures? Do you wonder that I have hired a private eye?"

"A — a private — eye?"

"Ah, to be sure," said he. "I must explain. That is what he calls himself in the vernacular. He is a sleuth, Christopher. I brought him from New York, where hardened criminals flee at the mere mention of his name."

Cat

I started to expostulate, but Witherspoon would brook no interruption. "I have arranged for you to meet him, to lunch with him. Not here, but secretly — at an establishment known, I believe, as Jakey's Java Joint."

"But, Bertrand," I protested feebly, "how can this person aid us? How?"

Witherspoon uttered a fierce, triumphant laugh. "Be patient, Christopher! Soon you will know all!"

I remember little of that first guarded meeting. Hulking, unshaven fellows wolfing their food in grubby cubicles, lewd language and coarse jests, vile music from an automatic instrument — all these I can recall only vaguely. My first unfavorable impression of Luigi Hogan, though, is still distinct. Small and round and surprisingly hairy, he neither looked nor behaved like a detective.

Witherspoon and I had turned up our coat collars and pulled our hat brims down to avoid recognition, but Hogan's sharp little eyes saw us immediately as we entered, and he greeted us with much pointless snickering. When he had pulled himself together, introductions were performed; and, in a moment, he and Witherspoon were plotting in undertones over thick cups of lukewarm coffee.

Hogan's diction was atrocious; his underworld argot was almost incomprehensible to me; he talked and laughed with his mouth full of salami sandwich. Even if our encounter with Cynthia Smithby had left me in full possession of my faculties, I doubt whether I could have gleaned more than occasional fragments of the conversation. I noticed that Hogan addressed Witherspoon as "Chief." I heard him say that he had been attending Smithby's extension course for animal trainers. I even caught the very words in which he recounted Smithby's advice to them: *Y'gotta show 'em you ain't afraid er nuttin', see? Y' gotta get right inner cages wit' 'em, see? Y' gotta talk t' them goddam big feelions like you was brudders.*

Witherspoon's expression became positively bloodthirsty at this point. "Hogan," he said, out of the corner of his mouth, "you go find us a circus or a zoo, see? With a good big vicious tiger, see? Heh heh! We'll challenge Mr. Smithby to go and reason with him in his cage. He can't refuse. Catch on?"

"I catch, Chief." Hogan snickered loathsomely. "Th' Press'll eat it up."

"Not just the Press," murmured Witherspoon with a ghoulish leer. "No indeed!"

As for the rest of what they said — well, he gave it to me in outline as we walked by obscure streets back to the campus. The idea of Smithby becoming an hors-d'oeuvre for a tiger was not their main plot. Hogan was to watch him constantly until he committed some dangerous indiscretion, preferably of an amorous nature. Then he was to secure photographs which we could use to disgrace Smithby, to procure his swift dismissal. As a last resort, he was to provide a person known as Marilynne, who had yet to meet failure in her career of breaking down male inhibitions.

Ordinarily, I would have been profoundly shocked by the utter ruthlessness of these methods. But now, aware only of Bogwood's dire plight, I shared Witherspoon's ferocity and felt no qualms. One thing alone perturbed me — Cynthia Smithby. True, she had no proper academic qualifications; the chance of her making any new discovery dangerous to us was remote indeed. Still, might not Smithby, after all, be nothing more than a red herring dragged by a shrewd, designing woman across our path?

Waiting for Hogan's labors to bear fruit was no easy task. Vain doubts and fears tormented me incessantly — and all the while things went from bad to worse. Against our bitter protests, a course in Feline Culture was added to the awful list. The Press, keeping *Cat* constantly in the public eye, greeted with laudatory reviews the appearance of Smithby's handbooks for zoo and circus personnel: *Basic Lion, Basic Leopard, Basic Panther,* and so on. And the columnists, meanwhile, harped on the rumored progress of Cynthia Smithby's project, the nature of which she was still keeping secret. It was, they hinted, a way of teaching *Cat* so simple that any child could learn it in an hour. Might it not, they asked, eliminate the need for baby-sitters, for kindergarten teachers? Might it not change the social and economic structure of the world?

We had our moments of encouragement. There was the day when Hogan was able to announce that he had made arrangements with a menagerie which owned a tiger, elderly and quite untameable, who had put an end to the earthly career of at least one trainer. The challenge had been mailed to Smithby. The newspapers had been informed. And you can well imagine that Witherspoon and I fairly jumped for joy when we saw the headlines. "CAT PROF MAY TAME FIERCE JUNGLE LORD!" they shouted.

But Smithby weaseled out of it. Chatting with any normal tiger, he announced, was most enjoyable. This was a different matter. This tiger was clearly psychopathic. "He needs a feline psychiatrist," said Smithby. "After all, even though I speak English, I would not try to reason with a human maniac armed to the teeth." And the servile Press praised him for his "hard common sense!"

The weeks dragged by, and our furtive meetings at Jakey's Java Joint brought more and more discouraging reports. Every small detail of Smithby's life was known — and irreproachable. Perversely, he insisted in behaving as a model husband. Even Marilynne, when finally we brought her from New York, found him quite unassailable. Even Marilynne, in whose hennaed presence poor Witherspoon blushed like any schoolboy, exercised her talents all in vain. With each attempt, her remarks became increasingly sarcastic, until eventually she abandoned us — leaving behind a note in which she suggested that a catnip mouse might bring us better luck.

Oddly enough, the collapse of Witherspoon's carefully contrived plans did not daunt him in the least; nor would he listen to my suggestion that henceforth we should fight Smithby on purely academic grounds. He insisted that we keep Hogan in our service; and, when I objected, he threatened to bring "goons" to settle Smithby's "hash."

Even when we learned that Smithby had complained against us to the Board of Regents, even when we were summoned to appear before that august body, he did not share my quickened fears and my despondency. "Ah, Christopher," he cried, shaking his fist, "on Friday we must go before the Board. That means we have three days! Believe me — something will turn up, and we will face the lot of them triumphantly. We will see Smithby crushed and broken yet. *Cat* will be nothing but an evil dream!"

How bitterly the jesting gods play cat-and-mouse with all that we hold dear! On Friday morning, drowned

Cat

in despair, I was making my hopeless way toward the campus when, to my astonishment, a large red cab came to a screeching stop beside me, and its door flew open to eject an exultant Witherspoon, who seized me by the arm.

"Victory is ours!" he trumpeted, pulling me to the vehicle. "Hogan just telephoned! Smithby is in our trap!" Before I could utter a word, he bundled me into the back seat ahead of him, and slammed the door. "Yip Lee's" he shouted to the driver, and we were off.

I got nothing further from him during that mad ride, for seemingly he knew no more. "I told you so, I told you so!" was the ecstatic cry with which he answered all my questions; and, when we reached our destination, a Chinese restaurant in the commercial district, I was as mystified as ever.

Leaving the cab and entering, we were greeted by a Celestial who spoke to Witherspoon by name. We were led upstairs to a small and private room. And there, upon its threshold, I saw a sight which took my breath away. In the center of the room stood a table and five chairs. Two of the chairs were empty. Two were occupied by Luigi Hogan and a well-dressed, middle-aged Chinese. On the fifth, covering his face in shame, sat Beowulf Yu.

As soon as he saw us, Hogan struck an attitude. "De whole t'ing's washed up, guys!" he declared. "All dis stuff about *Cat* — it's phony! Your Smit'by — he's a fake!"

I heard Witherspoon gasp; I heard a muffled sob from Beowulf Yu. "This is incredible!" I cried. "Why, I myself have heard him speak to cats. I've heard them answer back. Deplorable it is, yes — but surely it must be more than a mere web of fraud? Explain yourself, man."

Hogan began to quake with merriment. "It's — it's simple!" he giggled. "Shrimps!"

"*Shrimps?*" Witherspoon and I echoed the word with one voice.

But Hogan was too convulsed to answer. He jerked a thumb toward the Chinese gentleman beside him.

The Chinese smiled gravely. "That is correct," he said, bowing. "I, you see, am Chester Yu. I am the uncle of this dull youth —"With some distaste, he indicated Beowulf. "This dull youth with the absurd glasses, who has repaid me for bringing him to this country by failing to master even the rudiments of English. I am also the proprietor of the Pilgrim Fathers Seafood Market–"

He paused courteously while we took the vacant chairs. "For some time," he went on, "I had seen Professor Smithby come in regularly once a day, followed closely by Mr. Hogan. Furthermore, Professor Smithby always bought exactly ten cents worth of shrimps, refused to have them wrapped, and put them directly in his pocket. My curiosity was aroused — and, a day or so ago, I took the liberty of speaking to Mr. Hogan about it."

Hogan smirked.

"He and I compared notes. When I learned who my strange customer was, my interest redoubled. We Chinese, you know, revere learning, and my disreputable nephew's devotion to *Cat* had caused me much distress." Chester Yu's countenance assumed an expression of extreme severity. "Mr. Hogan and I came to the only possible conclusion. We tested our theory with Meow-Tse-Tung, my own pet cat; and the results were indisputable. He immediately became vocal at a whiff

Cat

of shrimp. So this morning we took Beowulf to task. Confronted by the evidence, he confessed all!"

Beowulf held his fingers to his ears, moaning softly.

"Yes," declared his uncle, "this wretched boy admitted that he had uncovered Smithby's secret, and turned it to his own dishonorable advantage. Smithby, you see, mewed at the cats — and the cats mewed for shrimp. There was no more to it than that."

"Do you mean," I exclaimed, "that all those people merely pretended to understand *Cat*?"

"Believing that Professor Smithby understood it perfectly, they feared to reveal what they regarded as their own stupidity."

I shook my head. "Surely no group of intelligent men and women — "

"Come, come, Christopher," protested Witherspoon, "I've seen the same sort of thing a dozen times in the Philosophy Department."

And I was forced to admit that he was right.

Then Witherspoon pushed his chair back and rose. "We are grateful to you, gentlemen," he asserted grimly, "for placing this monstrous swindler in our power. Now we can purge dear Bogwood of his presence, his mewing sycophants, and his nefarious works." He showed his teeth. "It is 11 o 'clock. In half an hour the Board of Regents meets — and you have earned the right to share our triumph, the triumph of true learning. Let us go! Let us grind vile Smithby in the dust!"

Without another word, he turned and strode toward the door; and we followed him, Chester Yu urging his weeping nephew forward with an ungentle hand. My heart was high indeed as we left the restaurant and entered Hogan's car.

The Timeless Tales of Reginald Bretnor

The Board of Regents was to meet, of course, in Cruett Hall, in the chamber dedicated by Ebenezer Bogwood to that purpose. It is a long room, panelled in ancient walnut, full of tradition's gentle gloom. Upon its walls hang the stern portraits of those scholars who, through the generations, have filled our presidential chair — and, as our small procession strode down the hall toward it, there came to me the thought of how their noble spirits would rejoice when Witherspoon and I pricked the miasmic bubble which was *Cat*.

My doubts were all dispelled. My fears had vanished. Like conquerors, we passed the bowing flunkey at the door —

Imagine, if you can, the sight which met our gaze. At the head of the great table, gaunt and gray, sat Mr. Sylvester Furnwillie, Chairman of the Board. At his right hand was seated the President of Bogwood; at his left, the loathsome Gregory Morton puffed at an opulent cigar. The six remaining Regents were ranged on either side. Beyond them, Smithby stood. Across from him, his wife reposed. And, at the table's very end, sat an enormous tomcat, staring at Mr. Furnwillie with cold, green eyes.

Smithby, all unaware of our entrance, was speaking. "... therefore," he was saying, "we observe that the *hsss-s-s* of Old *Cat* gradually changed to *fsss-t-t* in ordinary Modern *Cat*. That shows how simple the functioning of Grimalkin's Law can be —"

"Ha!" cried Witherspoon.

Smithby suddenly was still; all eyes were on us.

Mr. Furnwillie lifted his spectacles with a palsied hand. "Dear me, dear me!" he said uncertainly. "You are some minutes late, are you not? You really shouldn't

Cat

keep the Board of Regents waiting, gentlemen. No, indeed. Dr. Smithby has proferred some serious charges. Oh, *very* serious. He states that you have had him followed everywhere, and that you even hired a trollop to — er — seduce him. Tsk-tsk! We can't approve such goings-on at Bogwood, gentlemen, can we? After all—"

He broke off. He peered at Hogan and the Yus. His lofty forehead wrinkled with distaste. "Who are these people, Witherspoon? They cannot be alumni; they do not have the Bogwood look about them. Eh? Are they relatives of yours?"

Witherspoon folded his arms across his chest, and, in an awful voice, he answered, *"They are Smithby's doom!"*

There was a frightened murmur from the Regents. Gregory Morton emitted a vulgar feline expletive. Mr. Furnwillie exclaimed distractedly.

Witherspoon silenced them with one contemptuous glance. He pointed straight at Smithby. "Yes, his *doom!* We admit his charges, Flewkes and I! *We* hired Hogan to dog his wicked steps. *We* employed Marilynne. And we are proud of it — for by our humble efforts we have saved Bogwood from degradation and the world's disdain!"

Like Jove about to hurl his thunderbolt, he seemed to grow in stature standing there.

"Smithby!" he cried. "Smithby, your hour has come! Resign. Go far away. Never again befoul this sacred air! Beowulf has confessed your villainy, and we know all. We, Smithby, know about the shrimps!"

He paused. A dreadful silence reigned.

"Yes, the shrimps — the shrimps which Smithby conceals about his person, gentlemen!" Like a shrill trumpet, his voice shook the room. "*Cat* is a sham, a mockery, and a hollow fraud! No one can speak a single word of *Cat*! The creatures mew for — *Shrimp!*"

He stopped. We waited for the earth to open under Smithby's feet, the heavens to fall. And —

And nothing happened.

I looked. Dumbfounded, I looked again. Several of the Regents were whispering to each other and casting the most peculiar glances in our direction. Mr. Sylvester Furnwillie was conferring with Gregory Morton. Smithby and Cynthia Smithby were exchanging smiles. The large, striped tomcat was pretending to stare unconcernedly out the window.

"Wh-what does this mean?" demanded Witherspoon.

Mr. Furnwillie ignored him. He looked around. His countenance assumed an aspect of extreme displeasure. To me he said, "Professor Flewkes, though I am deeply shocked by this vindictive and absurd denunciation, it does not surprise me. It is in keeping with the questionable associates, the reprehensible activities. Such things we might expect of Witherspoon, for he is not originally a Bogwood man. But not of *you*. Tsk-tsk. I am most gravely disappointed. Indeed I am. You — well, you should be *ashamed*."

Shocked to the core, I started to protest. He did not let me.

"Professor Flewkes, we *know* about the shrimps. Of course Professor Smithby carries them, just as some men carry cigars to give their friends. Why shouldn't he? I carry them myself. Surely you don't expect a cat to smoke cigars?"

"B-but — but Beowulf —?" I stammered.

Cat

And it was Smithby who replied. "I think I can explain that," he said, a little sadly. "Not long ago, and much against my will, I was forced to tell poor Beowulf that I was flunking him. He was emotionally upset. I fear that, faced with his inability to master *Cat*, he sought refuge in the pretense that no one could."

Mr. Furnwillie thanked him. "You make it amply clear, Dr. Smithby — and I am only sorry that this incident should have marred so bright a morning"

Behind me I heard the voice of Chester Yu snap out an angry phrase in Cantonese. I heard a squeal of pain from Beowulf as he received some corporal punishment.

Mr. Furnwillie smiled. "When you have added such a glorious leaf to Bogwood's laurels..." His smile disappeared. "Yes, Professor Flewkes — this morning Dr. and Mrs. Smithby proved the validity of *Cat* to our complete satisfaction. They showed us the result of Mrs. Smithby's splendid project in education and research. Their proof is absolute, beyond cavil, and quite beyond the shadow of a doubt!"

"*You lie!*" screamed Witherspoon, livid with rage, trembling in every limb. "Don't try to tell me that this illiterate woman has taught each one of you to babble *Cat*! This is another fraud! And you are aiding and abetting it! I shall inform the Press! Hogan and I shall expose you for what you are!"

"Tsk-tsk!" Mr. Furnwillie said reprovingly. "If you behave like that, Witherspoon, you'll have to leave the room. I cannot babble *Cat, as* you so coarsely put it, but Mr. Morton can, and —"

Witherspoon whirled. "Come, Hogan, Flewkes! Let us seek the society of honest men!" He marched toward the door; and at the door he turned. "Furnwillie—" He roared defiance like a wounded lion. *"Furnwillie, I resign!"*

Then he was gone, with Hogan closely behind. The only sound was Hogan's foolish giggle in the corridor.

I lacked the strength to follow. Mutely, I stood before the Board, all my high hopes for Bogwood in ashes at my feet.

Mr. Furnwillie put on his spectacles and took them off again. "Dear me," he said, "how violent the man is! Even though Dr. and Mrs. Smithby, in their complaint, did ask us not to punish him, I fear that we must accept his resignation."

"Certainly!" growled Gregory Morton; and the other members of the Board nodded solemnly.

Mr. Furnwillie sighed. "Ah me, this leaves us with a painful duty, doesn't it? We should do something, I suppose, about Professor Flewkes?"

He looked at me, and so did all the rest. Even the tomcat favored me with a fixed regard.

I summoned all my shredded dignity. "Gentlemen," I answered, "I shall spare you this harsh necessity. I, too, shall seek a more congenial atmosphere."

And it was then that Cynthia Smithby, with a little cry, came to her feet and ran to me. "Dear Dr. Flewkes!" she pleaded, clinging to my arm. "Do not resign! Why, Emerson and I are both so fond of you — we could not bear the thought. I beg you, stay! Let us convince you."

As the impassioned words poured forth, she drew me willy-nilly toward the table's end.

"Let us open to you our brave new world, where cats can take at last their rightful place, contributing to science, culture, and the arts. Believe me — you will see

Cat

the day when cats shall vote, hold public office, and instruct our youth. Perhaps there even may be peace on earth under a parliament of Man and Cat!"

She pointed at the tomcat on his chair. "Look! Only look! This is Rabindranath. He's the living proof!"

Roughly, I shook her off. "Madam," I exclaimed, "I am no fool. You may delude your students. You may deceive Mr. Furnwillie in his senility. But you can not persuade me that you can teach a language which does not exist!"

"Oh *please*," she implored, "I do assure you — you do not understand. I'll introduce you to Rabindranath. His interests lie within your own domain. He's starting to translate The Aspern Papers into Cat. Dear Dr. Flewkes, at least will you not speak with him? Will you not converse?"

Two tears flowed like dewdrops down her cheeks. They did not move me. "Converse?" Contemptuously, I gestured at the cat. "No, never! Never will I demean myself to — *mew!*"

And — ah, cruel gods!

Coolly, Rabindranath looked me up and down. "Mew?" he said. "That will be scarcely necessary."

2
Maybe Just a Little One

This was the first of Bretnor's short stories to be published. It appeared in Harper's Magazine *in August, 1947. It was later reprinted in* The Magazine of Fantasy & Science Fiction *in February, 1953. The story appeared later in a book,* The Best from Fantasy and Science Fiction, Third Series, *put out in hardcover by Doubleday & Co. in February, 1954, and in paperback by Ace Books in 1960. The story was also published by magazines in Great Britain, France and Spain. It was included as well in Bretnor's book,* One Man's BEM: Thoughts on Science Fiction, *published by The Borgo Press in both hard and soft cover in 1990.*

Maximus Everett, who taught physics at Woodrow Wilson Union High School for nearly twenty years, was the first man to accomplish nuclear fission in his basement.

It really wasn't much of a basement either. Along one side was the workbench, littered with tools and wire and dusty old books. On the other side was an empty birdcage and a utility sink with a dripping faucet. A couple of shabby trunks stood in a corner next to a broken lawnmower, and some baled magazines the Red Cross people had forgotten to call for were piled up behind the cyclotron.

The final result of his scientific labors pleased Everett. After observing it quietly for a while, he went

Maybe Just a Little One

upstairs to the kitchen, where his wife was making chopped-olive-and-egg sandwiches. He sat down on a stool, wiped his long bald forehead, and remarked that it certainly was hot in the basement.

Without turning around, his wife assured him that this was not abnormal. "Here in Arizona," she observed, "right near the border, it's always hot in summer."

Everett did not dispute the point. "Oh, it's not only that," he told her. "I've just been working pretty hard. It's been a tough job." He leaned back with a little sigh of satisfaction. "I've invented atomic power, hon."

"So that's what you've been doing," said Mrs. Everett. "I thought you were still working on your perpetual motion machine." She cut the last sandwich diagonally in half, put some sliced pickle on the platter, and turned around, smoothing her ample apron. Then suddenly she looked accusingly at her husband. "Why, that's ridiculous!" she exclaimed. "What do you mean, *you* invented it? How about Hiroshima?"

"That was different," said Everett simply. "That was just a big bang. Anybody can invent that kind."

Mrs. Everett—a librarian, and rather dogmatic—showed signs of irritation. "All the *authorities*," she declared, "say that you have to have uranium, and that it's very rare. Then you have to make it into something else, and it costs millions and millions of dollars."

"That's what *they* think," replied Everett, shaking his head mildly.

"Well, they ought to know, if anyone does!"

"I have the utmost respect for them," he conceded. "After all, their work did help to make mine possible. It's just—well, you see, it's just that I don't need uranium. I discovered a new element about a week ago, and...."

Mrs. Everett was wearing the expression she usually reserved for people who tried to explain away overdue books. "Just *how* could you discover a new element when they've all *been* discovered?" she asked bleakly. "And what is it called?"

"*Frijolium*," Everett replied. "I discovered it a week ago Tuesday. And it hardly costs anything."

"Yes, but where did you get it?"

"I made it. That is, I purified it. Pure frijolium, for the first time in history."

"Well, it sounds sort of familiar to me," mused Mrs. Everett. "Frijolium—now wherever...?"

"Sort of familiar?" Everett echoed. "Well, it should! Frijolium. You know, from *frijoles*."

Marriage and the public library had hardened Mrs. Everett; she took it all in her stride. "*Max*imus Everett!" she snapped. "Do you mean to sit there and tell me that you've found a new element in plain old Mexican beans?"

Everett hooked his thumbs in his belt and tilted the stool back on its hind legs. "We-ell," he said, obviously weighing the question carefully, "it would not be quite correct to say that frijoles *contain* a new element. As a matter of fact, they *are* the new element."

"But frijoles are just beans!" protested Mrs. Everett, rather loudly. "Anybody'll tell you that. They contain proteins, fats, and carbohydrates."

"Those substances," Everett said, "are impurities. Fresh frijoles are 92.733 per cent pure frijolium. I have isolated it. It has a relatively low atomic weight, but is adequately unstable. The nucleus may be split quite readily by...."

"Oh, never mind!" Mrs. Everett cried, stamping her foot. "Do you really expect me to believe that? Why, there would have been an explosion."

"No, there wouldn't. I didn't want an explosion. I used the frijolium from one small frijole—that's the minimum critical mass—and it's really quite easy to control. You can turn it on and off just like a vacuum-cleaner."

"Well, I don't believe a word of it! All the experts say atomic power can't be controlled like that."

Everett shook his head, pityingly. "That's what *they* think. I've had it running the washing-machine for three hours.... And," he added, "if I didn't turn it off, it would run for almost exactly seventy-two years. What do you think of that?"

After this, of course, Mrs. Everett followed him back into the basement to see for herself. The washing-machine was busily churning away next to the cyclotron, quaking and rattling just as it always had. Mrs. Everett sniffed. Warily, she walked around it, peering at the chipped enamel of its framework. As far as she could determine, its appearance had not changed—and she said so rather acidly.

"If this is your idea of a joke," she said. "I don't think it's at all funny. Of course, if you haven't broken my washer, there's no real harm done, but...."

Everett interrupted her. He pointed to the back of the washer. "Look!" he said, with great dignity.

Looking closely, she saw a small aluminum box, with a round hole in the top and an insulated cord leading to the motor. "Wasn't it there before?" she asked.

"It was not!" Everett said. "That is the generator. You drop the frijolium through the hole. That little switch on the box works a shield inside that turns the energy on and off." He flipped the switch, and the washing-machine chugged twice and was silent. He flipped it again, and the machine came back to life.

"See?" he said triumphantly.

Mrs. Everett was still dubious. "Where do you plug it in?" she inquired.

"You don't," her husband replied patiently. "That's the whole idea. The generator converts atomic power from the smashing of the frijolium nuclei directly into 110 volts A.C., just like the house current."

"You—you mean we won't have any bills to pay?" Mrs. Everett said, beginning to be impressed.

"Not a penny. Not after I get the rest of the house wired."

"Why, Maxie! Why, that's wonderful! And we could put it on the car too, couldn't we?" Mrs. Everett patted the washing-machine with genuine affection. "Just wait until I tell Mrs. Myers," she exulted. "Ever since they made Henry principal, she's been acting as if we were below them socially or something. And it was she who told the grocer-boy that you were all thumbs, not handy around the house like Henry was."

"Oh, Henry's all right," Everett said. "I think he'll be pleased when he hears about it. After all, it'll be nice for the school, too; it'll help to keep up interest in the physics classes."

"I should think he ought to be pleased," snorted Mrs. Everett. "*He* couldn't invent atomic power."

"Maybe," Everett said wistfully, "maybe he'll let me give up coaching basketball."

Maybe Just a Little One

"I'll phone her right after lunch," Mrs. Everett said with a gleam in her eye.

Mrs. Everett was as good as her word. She was sweetly condescending to Henry Myers' wife, who responded with a gratifying display of irritation, awe, and envy—and this reaction encouraged her to call up quite a number of other people. It was Saturday, and she didn't have to go back to the library, and so she was able to spend the rest of the afternoon on the telephone. She was still there at five o'clock, when the reporters started to arrive.

The first journalist was a brash young man with an unhealthy complexion. "I'm from the *Bulletin*," he announced, cleverly getting his foot in the door as Mrs. Everett opened it.

"There must be some mistake," Mrs. Everett said coldly. "We paid the boy two months in advance, and anyway we take the *Tribune*."

"No mistake," said the journalist. "Here's the card." He thrust a card at her menacingly and, as she retreated, thrust himself after it, craning his neck to peer around the room. "Where's the guy with the atom bomb?" he demanded.

"Oh, you're a reporter!" Mrs. Everett said, wide-eyed.

"Where's the atom bomb?" repeated the journalist, peering into the fireplace.

"Atom bomb?" gasped Mrs. Everett. "Dear me, no. There isn't any. It's just atomic power. It's running the washing-machine."

The journalist seemed disappointed. "You sure?" he said.

The Timeless Tales of Reginald Bretnor

"Why, of course," replied Mrs. Everett. "Maximus—that's Mr. Everett—will be here in a minute or two. He'll explain it to you. If you'll just have a seat for a minute, I'll go and get him." She started out. "If you'd like to look at the new *Geographic*," she offered, "it's on the mantel."

The journalist grunted politely as she left the room. Then he took a quick look at the bookcase, discovered two volumes by Jules Verne and one by H.G. Wells, noted down their titles. Having done so, he opened the door for his cameraman, and together they began examining Everett's desk for matters of scientific interest.

The Everetts, entering, did not notice this investigation; they were momentarily blinded by the flash-bulb that greeted their return. Everett tried simultaneously to rearrange his hastily-assumed necktie with one hand and to shake hands with the journalist with the other, and succeeded in looking quite confused and slightly wild.

Mrs. Everett blinked and said something about how clever Mr. Everett was. The journalist promptly asked about the atomic bomb again, and did not conceal his resentment when Everett assured him that there was nothing so dangerous in the house. He slumped down into the nearest chair, muttered indignantly that he had flown down from Phoenix, flipped his notebook closed. "Well," he said to Everett, "give."

And, modestly enough, Everett gave. He told of his search for practical atomic power. He exhibited his home-made cyclotron and the converted washer. He posed for a dozen or more photographs, and he answered all questions with the utmost patience. "Of

Maybe Just a Little One

course," he said, "I could have made a bomb if I'd wanted to, but I think this is so much more useful, don't you?"

The journalist made a note of this remark. "Yeah," he said, "sure. But all the big shots say it can't be done for ten or twenty years."

Everett grinned. "That's what *they* think," he said. "You see, they haven't heard about my new element. It's the new element that does the trick. And it hardly costs anything; that's the nice thing about it."

The journalist poised his pencil.

"I call it frijolium," Everett continued. "From frijoles, you know."

The journalist's face twitched suddenly. He darted a quick, covert glance at his companion. "No kiddin'!" he said, with a nasty smile. "You mean it comes from frijoles—from *beans*?"

"That's right," Everett assured him. "From common old Mexican beans. They're full of it."

"Say, that's something! That's really something!" The journalist slapped Everett heartily on the back. "Isn't that *something*, Pete?" he cried.

Pete took another photograph.

The first journalist didn't stay very long after that. He remembered that he was in a terrific hurry, and he delayed only long enough to use the telephone very briefly. Mrs. Everett, overhearing part of the conversation, marvelled at the strange jargon of his craft.

"...Yeah," he said, "...uh-huh, a squirrel... but good!... sure... runs the washer on frijolium... from frijoles... you heard what I said, as in beans!... Willie'll eat it up...."

But that was all Mrs. Everett heard, because just then the other journalists started to arrive.

There were a lot of them, male and female, and they gave the Everetts a very busy evening. As a matter of fact, it was two-and-a-half hours past midnight when the last journalist—a heavily-mustached lady who had been questioning Mrs. Everett about the more intimate details of her married life—folded her notes and departed.

After the door had been securely bolted, a strangely demure Mrs. Everett looked up at her husband. "Oh, Maxie," she fluttered, "that woman asked me the most embarrassing questions."

"Dear me," Everett said uncomfortably. "I wonder why?"

There was a moment of silence. Then Mrs. Everett sighed. "Well anyhow, you'll probably be quite famous now," she suggested. "They... they may even ask you to go to Washington."

"That would be nice," Everett said, "but I don't see how I possibly could before the end of the semester."

Mentally reading future headlines, Mrs. Everett ignored the objection. She glimpsed a brief and garbled vision of honorary degrees, speeches, movie contracts. "All those newspaper people were so disappointed because you hadn't made a bomb," she reflected. "It does seem a shame, too, after they went to all that trouble. Don't you think you could make just *one*? Maybe just a little one...."

"No," Everett replied. "I'd rather not. I don't like to seem obstinate, but whatever would we do with it?"

The Everetts were given no chance to stay in bed that Sunday morning, for the press returned in force on the heels of the milkman, and soon the household was

Maybe Just a Little One

as agitated as it had been the night before. The telephone was constantly in use; light-hearted journalists came and went; and Mrs. Everett whispered a thousand confidences to ladies who knew just how to contrive high romance from the most unpromising materials.

At fifteen minutes to twelve, Maximus Everett was perched on the pile of old magazines in the basement, rather hoarsely lecturing on the peculiar merits of the frijole as a fissionable material, while several members of his audience examined and photographed an assortment of rusty plumbing installed for an experiment long since abandoned and forgotten. It was here that Mrs. Everett found him when she descended the stairs to announce the arrival of Henry Myers.

"I do hate to interrupt," Mrs. Everett said delicately but firmly, "but could you come upstairs for a minute, dear? There's *someone* to see you."

"Tell him to come down," Everett replied. "I'll start over again so he won't miss anything."

"But it's *Henry*!" protested Mrs. Everett, leaning out over the rickety railing. "He says it's important!"

Everett came suddenly alive. "Henry?" he cried. "I told you so! He's changed his mind about my coaching basketball. I'll be right up. Tell him I'll be right up! Boys," he said to the journalists, "do you mind waiting down here? Just browse around. I won't be a second."

"Go right ahead," they answered, as one man. And they followed Everett enthusiastically as he took the stairs three at a time.

Henry Myers was waiting in the living room, standing with his broad back to the fireplace. He held his hat in one hand, a folded newspaper and an envelope in the other. His eyebrows slanted down toward the bridge of his nose with administrative severity—and they relaxed neither at Everett's entrance nor at his hearty greeting.

"Henry, old boy!" At the head of his escort, Everett swept across the carpet with outstretched hand. "I'm sure glad to see you! Come on down and...."

And then Maximus Everett was checked in full career. Henry Myers spoke. His voice was sharp and metallic, an unkind voice, the voice of a man who for years has dealt none too gently with refractory adolescents.

"Everett," he said, "I had hoped to see you privately; I see that privacy is impossible. However, I anticipated such a contingency. I came prepared, and I shall do what is necessary without further discussion." He thrust the newspaper and the envelope into Everett's welcoming hand. "One," he declared, "will explain the other."

Then he turned on his heel, jammed his hat on, angrily brushed aside two questing newsmen—and the front door banged behind him.

Now, quite understandably, this interview knocked Maximus Everett slightly off-center. He stared open-mouthed at the quivering door, only remotely conscious of a buzz of voices, of questions being asked, of objects in his hand—until a voice more strident than the rest made itself heard.

"Let's see!" it shouted. "Let's take a look! Take a look, Maxie!"

So Everett looked. Mechanically, he started to unfold the newspaper, recalling vaguely that it was the first he had seen since his discovery was made public. As the black headlines appeared, there was a sudden hush.

Maybe Just a Little One

At first, Everett only realized that he was reading about himself; though the meaning was seeping through, he was still protected against its full import.

WHOOPS! yelled the headlines gaily, BEAN ATOM BUSTED.

Below that, two lines of smaller type proclaimed:

Frijole Fission Runs Washer for Basement Einstein: Clean Undies Prove Plutonium Now Obsolete.

And there, to illustrate the point, was a picture of the Everetts, grinning idiotically as they displayed the significant article of apparel against the side of the cyclotron.

Still functioning mechanically, Everett by-passed the caption to find the story:

> Mighty forces—[he read]—which Arizona's old-timers have always suspected to lie lurking in the redoubtable Mexican frijole have at last been liberated, according to Maximum Everett, high school physics teacher and self-proclaimed basement genius of Concho County, who yesterday took the wraps off his home-grown Oak Ridge project for the first time and let everybody in on the swell new world now looming up (says he) on the bean horizon....

Numbed as he was, Everett might very well have gone on to read the rest of the story, but just then some more black type, off to one side, caught his notice:

BEAN-BUSTER MAXIE NO COLD FISH, SAYS MRS.
Atomic Love Brings...

But that was as far as Everett got. Full comprehension, long delayed, hit him with a solid rabbit-punch. The paper fell from his fingers to the floor. A large round tear, forming at the corner of his eye, began to slide slowly down his cheek.

The Timeless Tales of Reginald Bretnor

Observing these phenomena, Everett's audience found it expedient to melt away, motivated perhaps by delicacy, perhaps by an intuitive appreciation of the fact that the really worthwhile part of the show was over. One by one, unnoticed by their host, they made their departure, until only two or three of the unregenerate were left. These waited patiently until Everett recovered enough to open Henry Myers' letter. Then they read it over his shoulder, finding it brief and to the point:

> My Dear Mr. Everett:
>
> In view of the scandalous events of the past two days, the Board of Trustees has instructed me to notify you of the termination of your contract. The Board is granting you an extended leave of absence (without pay) until the end of the present semester, at which time the termination will take effect.
>
> The Members of the Board and I agree that, under the circumstances, no additional explanation of this action can be necessary.
>
> Very sincerely yours,
>
> *Henry T. Myers*
>
> Henry T. Myers, Principal

Nobody said anything. After a moment, Everett carefully folded the letter again and returned it to its envelope. Then he walked to the door and held it open until the last of his remaining visitors had filed out, and only when it was locked behind them did he permit himself a brief outburst of emotion. He tore the letter in half. He threw it on the floor. He said, "That's what *you* think!" angrily several times.

Maybe Just a Little One

Bean-Buster Maxie was a nine-day wonder. The press, finding him suddenly uncooperative, confined its efforts to questioning friends and neighbors, fell back on its already large store of photographs, and explained the working of the Everett washer by hinting broadly at hidden wiring and compressed air. Before fresher wonders forced frijole back through the want-ads into oblivion, its every aspect had been thoroughly explored. There had been several jolly interviews with lesser physicists, several with screen and radio comedians, one with the spiritual leader of a vegetarian cult, and one with a rather bawdy admiral.

But the giants of the scientific and political worlds had held themselves aloof, refraining from all comment. The powers-that-be had not summoned Everett to Washington. No academic senates had honored him. No universities had invited him to join their faculties. Even the FBI, hastily checking up on all known foreign agents and finding them uninterested, had dropped him from its social register.

During the weeks that followed this brief period of international notoriety, the Everetts kept very much to themselves, scarcely stirring out of the house, and greeting even their oldest friends with a frigid reserve. Everett buried himself in his work, first converting the house-circuit to frijolium-power, then installing a generator in the family car.

Mrs. Everett, who had resigned from the Public Library after a determined but futile resistance, was his constant companion; and many were the long evenings they spent together, reading Walt Whitman aloud and making nebulous plans for a frijolium factory. Even after small boys stopped hooting at Everett in the street, they hesitated to venture far abroad; only the inexorable operation of economic law finally forced them out of the fancied security of their retreat.

Everett had never been too provident a man, and people of moderate means who invest in cyclotrons — no matter how small — seldom retain respectable bank balances. After about two months, Everett started job-hunting. He hunted in person and he hunted by mail, and he found both methods equally fruitless. Whatever he tried, there were — curiously enough — no vacancies. Once he was offered temporary employment as a sheepherder, but this was while he still was relatively solvent, and the chance did not come along again.

In six more weeks, the Everetts found themselves reduced to exactly 70 cents in cash and a dubious charge account. They discovered this just after lunch, and they moved to the living-room to discuss the matter.

"All this would never have happened," said Mrs. Everett bitterly, "if it hadn't been for that Henry Myers. I warned you against him the first day you met him, Maximus."

"Oh, Henry's not so bad," Everett protested. "It wasn't his fault, dear, I'm sure. The press just treated the whole thing with such a complete lack of understanding." He shrugged. "Well, I guess we'll just have to take out a second mortgage to tide us over. I hate to do it, but…"

"What?" cried Mrs. Everett. "And stay in *this* town? I'd sooner scrub floors! We ought to sell the place, and go away to…"

But Mrs. Everett was not fated to reveal her intended destination, for at that instant the doorbell rang. It rang once; then it rang again. It was starting its third

Maybe Just a Little One

summons when Everett opened the door, blinked into the sunlight, and found himself looking at three strangers — all of whom were dark and obviously foreign.

"What do you want?" Everett demanded rudely.

There was a tall dark man with a mustache and a black Homburg hat. There was a small dark man with a mustache and a black Homburg. There was a very large dark man with neither.

The tall dark man bowed profoundly over his stick and gloves; so did his small companion. The very large dark man kept his hands in his pockets and looked straight ahead.

"Do I address Doctor Everett?" inquired the tall dark man with grave courtesy and a marked accent.

Everett, who had obtained his B.A. with some little difficulty, was pleased in spite of himself. He blushed, cleared his throat, and coughed affirmatively.

"Then permit me to introduce myself," said the tall dark man, handing him a visiting card.

Everett took the card. *Antonio L. MacJones*, he read, *Ph.D., LL.D. (Columbia '22), Minister of the Interior, The Raptarian Republic.*

"Won't you come in?" Everett mumbled.

Once inside, the Minister of the Interior presented his colleague. "This," he announced, "is our General Troppo. In our country, he is Minister of— of Education."

The general clicked his heels and bowed.

"Education?" Everett asked suspiciously. "And he's a general?"

The Minister of the Interior explained that in his tranquil land military rank was largely honorary. "…in memory of our great liberator, who died in battle 112 years ago," he added.

The Timeless Tales of Reginald Bretnor

Everybody sat down except the very large dark man, who stood with his hands in his pockets, and kept peering out of the windows. There was some further exchange of formalities, with flowery Raptarian solicitude for the good health, past, present, and future, of Mr. and Mrs. Maximus Everett. Then the Minister of the Interior spoke at length about what his government was doing for the Common Man, and about a President so well-beloved that no other had been elected for nearly 30 years — and throughout his speech the dove of peace cooed a gentle obbligato.

The Everetts were enthralled. They saw the peaks and plains, the lush groves and verdant jungles of Raptaria. They beheld the clean, hard-working Raptarian peasant leading his chubby children to a new and splendidly-appointed school provided by a government whose watchwords were Benevolence and Progress.

The Minister of the Interior paused, and the Everetts sighed longingly — and as they did so he rose suddenly to his feet, lifting a hand to heaven.

"That is why we are here today," he cried out. "So that you, Maximo Everett, can aid us in our great humane task! In our country we have a physicist, a good man. He tells us that his work confirms your wonderful discovery. Already we have formed a Frijole Control Commission! — Come to us! Though we are poor, you will have everything you need. You will be Vice-Minister of Education. You will work directly under General Troppo!"

Having finished, the Minister of the Interior opened his arms in a magnificent gesture of ardent welcome, bowed, and sat down, quite winded by his exertions.

Maybe Just a Little One

"Ah, not under me!" expostulated General Troppo with equal fervor. "Not under me! Say rather as a colleague, a comrade!" He smiled, radiating good fellowship. "Of course," he said to Everett, "you can make explosives?"

Everett frowned, but before he had a chance to reply Mrs. Everett answered for him. "Mr. Everett could make an atomic bomb just as easy as pie," she told the general, "but he doesn"t want to. He thinks they're very destructive, and he can't see any point to making them."

Everett nodded vigorously while the Raptarian dignitaries exchanged swift glances; then the Minister of the Interior stepped into the breach with hearty laughter. "My friend!" he exclaimed, as soon as his amusement had subsided. "My very good friend! I fear that you mistake the general's meaning! What use would we, in poor Raptaria, ever have for an atomic bomb? But we have mines in our mountains. We must build dams across our so-swift rivers. We need many roads and bridges. That is the kind of explosives the Minister of Education means — for blasting! Is that not so, General?"

"Yes, yes," the general said hastily —

"But of course," smiled the Minister of the Interior, "for that — and for our national holiday, when the happy people celebrate with fireworks. That is why we may want a very few explosives, though we want power-plants even more."

"Power-plants?" echoed General Troppo. "Yes, yes."

"We-ell," Everett said, scratching his head, "I guess that is sort of different." He hesitated. "I... I won't have to coach basketball, will I?" he asked diffidently.

Some time has passed since the Everetts went to the Republic of Raptaria. As Vice-Minister of Education, Everett naturally did not have to bother with any of the details of his departure. Everything, including a Raptarian passport for two, had been arranged by the Minister of the Interior, and it all went off very smoothly — so smoothly, in fact, that for a long time even the Everetts' neighbors did not know that they had moved out of town permanently. Nobody ever dreamed that they had gone abroad.

Nobody. Not even Henry Myers, who happened to mention the Raptarian Republic when he delivered his weekly speech on world affairs in the assembly hall of Woodrow Wilson Union High School a few days ago.

"...and by contrast," he informed the student body, "we have news of another quiet, orderly election in Raptaria, a little country many of you may not even have heard about."

He paused, to smile benignly at the upturned faces. "A lucky little country, too," he told them. "Too small to worry about the great quarrels that rend the world. Too poor," he continued, "to follow any ways but those of peace."

That's what *he* thinks.

3
Unknown Things

"Unknown Things" was first published in Twilight Zone *magazine in February, 1989. It was reprinted the following year in* The Year's Best Fantasy and Horror, *edited by Ellen Datlow and Terri Windling, St. Martin's Press, New York.*

I have met any number of collectors during my thirty years in the antique trade: greedy ones (though, of course, they're all greedy one way or another), and some with superb taste and a deep understanding of their fields, some with book knowledge and no taste at all, others who collect status symbols or security blanks, rare people with whom it is a joy to converse and many more utter bores, and others still so unbelievably eccentric that they defy classification. But Andreas Hoogstraten was the strangest of them all. Always polite, almost always smiling, he still seemed to carry with him that eerie coldness you find in haunted houses. Neither his obvious wealth nor his perfect tailoring, neither his patrician nose, sleek blond hair, and thick, impossibly yellow eyebrows, nor a voice as soft and gentle as a cooing dove's could conceal it, at least from me.

I met him first in a Glastonbury pub. Every year, I'd go to England, buy an ancient van, and spend two months at least driving around and about, through Scotland and back down to Wales and Cornwall, buying big antiques and filling them with little antiques, then for the last third of my time crossing over to the continent and doing the same thing in France and the Low Countries. When the van was full, I'd ship it back as deckload on a freighter—this was in the days when you could do that—and drive it home to Saybrook from wherever it landed. It was a lot of fun, and I enjoyed every bit of it.

The Glastonbury pub was called the Weeping Nun—after some local ghost story—with an eighteenth-century sign that showed its dismal subject against a background of ancient tombstones and a silver moon—but inside it was the essence of English country hospitality, with all the dark wood and pewter and hunting prints you might expect, a great fireplace fit for roasting haunches of beef but cold now in the summertime, and neither a jukebox nor a telly to ruin the atmosphere. I went there with a local dealer, Tod Bardsley, with whom I had done business for several years, and we were just about to have lunch when Hoogstraten came in. He waved. He strode over to our table, carrying his cold aura with him.

"Mr. Bardsley, they said you'd be here, but I see you're with a friend?"

Bardsley nudged my foot under the table. He moved over. "Ah, do sit down, Mr. Hoogstraten," he invited. "Charles here won't mind. He's a fellow dealer," he chuckled, "always happy to meet another customer, like all of us."

We were introduced. I shook Hoogstraten's tense, cold hand. I was, I said, pleased to meet him. I was indeed a dealer, but I was a long way from home.

Briefly, Bardsley told him about my yearly trips, while the girl brought us two half-and-halfs and took his order for a whiskey and soda.

Unknown Things

"You really must get around," he commented, looking at me intently. "I imagine you see a far greater variety of things than the average dealer, don't you?"

"Rather!" Bardsley laughed. "There's not a shop from Land's End to John O' Groat's Charlie's not been in, to say nothing of across Channel. I daresay he's probably seen a thing or two that'd strike your fancy."

"What do you collect," I asked.

He turned his head, and I found myself looking directly into his lashless eyes. They were almost a matte blue, reminding me of Wedgwood Jasper ware, and they looked dry, as though they'd never known tears.

"What do I collect?" he said. "As our friend here will tell you, I buy anything I do not understand. I do not mean the expert's understanding of antiques and works of art. If I do not know what a thing is, if I cannot imagine what it was made for, it intrigues me, and if it's for sale I buy it. You see, if I do not know, and if nobody can tell me, it makes me determined to find out, to solve the problem. Where is your shop?"

"In Saybrook, in Connecticut."

"Well, that's certainly near enough to me. My apartment's in New York."

We exchanged cards, and he said he'd take a run up one of these days and have a look around and made me promise to keep my eyes peeled for any of his mysterious objects. He was, he told me, on his way to Istanbul and the Near East generally, and perhaps to Nepal and, now that the Chinese were letting down the barriers, to Tibet.

Shortly after our lunch arrived, he rose to go, saying he'd see Bardsley later at the shop, and once more he made me promise to look out for him.

He left, and I asked Tod about him.

"He's a rum one, Charlie. Buys anything if you can't tell him what it is, and pays well too. Last time in my place, he saw a weird cast-iron tool with a lot of cogs and a twisty handle that somehow didn't seem to connect with anything. He peered at it and peered at it, and finally took it with him looking like the cat fresh from the cream jug. A year or so back, too, I found him a painting—a dark thing like something seventeenth-century Dutch—but not like any you ever saw. The more you tried to make out what the subject was, the odder it looked. But it was done by a real artist, you could tell that. He paid me seven hundred without a quiver. And the real beauty of it is, he buys things that otherwise you'd have on hand forever—so what if he is strange looking, with those crazy eyebrows and blue-blue eyes?"

I told him then about the coldness, but he said the man had never affected him that way, so I put the thought aside as a quirk of my own.

Now I know that it was not.

Actually, Hoogstraten never did take the trouble to come up to Saybrook and visit my shop, and for three or four months I almost forgot about him. Then, at a flea market, I found a gadget I couldn't make head or tail of—one which ordinarily I'd have passed by without a second look. It was beautifully made of brass and polished steel, and its fitted mahogany box clearly went back to the last decade of the nineteenth century. Cased with it were eight or ten brass wheels, the rim of each serrated with geometrical neatness and with its individual pattern. It had a central axis to which these might have been affixed, a plunger like a date-stamp's, a spirit level,

Unknown Things

and two calibrated dials the purpose of which I couldn't even guess at. The man who had it thought it might have been a check-writing device, but he couldn't tell me how it possibly could have worked.

I bought the thing for less than twenty dollars, and that night I phoned Hoogstraten and was pleased to find him back from his journeyings. I described it to him, and instantly his voice came alive with interest. No, he couldn't possibly come up to Saybrook, not then, but would I bring it to New York?

I hesitated, for it seemed like quite an expedition for what I assumed would be a pretty petty deal, and at once he answered my unspoken question. "You needn't worry about the money part, Mr. Dennison—it is Dennison, isn't it? I am accustomed to paying well for anything that meets my criteria—at least in three figures—unless, of course, the seller has already set a lower price. In this case, even if I do not buy it, I'll make the trip worth your while."

So I agreed to bring it to him on the Sunday, and he gave me an address near Sutton Place—his card had carried only his phone number. The cab dropped me off at two in the afternoon in front of a several-story, obviously very expensively converted brownstone, with a martial doorman mounting guard at the entrance. I waited humbly while he made his phone call, and saw that there was only a single flat on each floor.

"Mr. Hoogstraten is waiting for you," he told me finally, giving my shoes and sports coat a supercilious farewell appraisal. "Take the elevator to the third floor."

The elevator was smooth and swift and new, and I was whisked to my destination in an instant. There a man-servant was waiting for me—I won't say a butler.

The Timeless Tales of Reginald Bretnor

He was short and muscular and massive, with a pale square face and huge hands. I judged him to be some sort of general factotum—chauffeur perhaps? Guard? He looked more like a hit-man. But he was polite enough, bowing me through the hall and opening the door for me.

I don't know exactly what I had expected, but it was not the Museum of Modern Art decor that greeted me, spare and stark and rectilinear, self-consciously manipulating mass and light and shadow in grays and blacks, startling whites, intrusive yellows, solid reds, some of the furniture echoing it, some tortured, twisted, with a thin scattering of anomalous ornaments. Of the objects he collected, there was no sign.

My face, I know, must have mirrored my astonishment, but he did not notice. He had eyes only for the package I was carrying, and I saw how hard his small black pupils were in their Wedgwood settings. He did not ask me to sit down. Dressed like something from a *Vanity Fair* men's fashions ad, he seized it without a word, opened it. His lips now drawn back from his almost too even teeth, he plucked the gadget from its box, hastily put the box down on a table, seated himself. For several minutes, he examined it, testing this, trying that, while I stood there uncomfortably.

Finally, "What do you suppose it is?" he asked.

"I haven't the foggiest," I answered. "The man I bought it from thought it might have been intended as some sort of check protector."

He said that was nonsense, and went back to his examination for several more long, silent minutes.

Then he looked up at me. He smiled, and again I felt wrapped in coldness. "It is satisfactory," he told me.

Unknown Things

"Yes, it is completely satisfactory. I shall derive pleasure from it." He nodded. "Indeed yes. Will five hundred be adequate?"

"You are very generous," I said, accepting the five hundred-dollar bills.

And at that point, a door opened and a woman entered. The effect was unbelievable. She paused, regarding us—and suddenly, as far as I was concerned, no one else was in the room. Her presence dominated it. She was tall, her hair coal black, as were her eyes. Her cheekbones were high. But the physical details were nothing compared with the totality. Suddenly I knew why men had imagined goddesses, and sacrificed to them, why there had been tilting in the lists and knightly quests, why late Victorian artists like Burne-Jones had so idealized the beauty of womankind. And simultaneously there was another surge, one I still feel when I remember her, that very natural one that sets your loins afire.

She turned toward us, and against all reason I was quite sure that she did not walk, but flowed, floated. Nor was she gowned for any such effect. She was dressed simply, in a tailored suit with white lace at the throat, and almost no jewelry; a brooch, a wedding ring.

Hoogstraten looked up, frowning slightly. "You're going out?" he asked.

"Yes, dear," she answered—and at the word irrational jealousy flamed in me. "Only for a—how do you say it?—for an hour or two perhaps? You do not need me here?"

She had the strangest accent I've ever heard, one I was quite unable to identify. All I can say is that somehow, to my ear, it sounded archaic.

He didn't even answer, his attention once more on the thing I'd sold him.

"Good-bye," she said, smiled very slightly at me, and left.

I had to interrupt him. "Mrs. Hoogstraten?" I asked.

"Yes, yes," he replied, a hint of irritation in his voice. "Pretty, isn't she?"

She's magnificent! I thought. But I had sense enough not to say it. It took him a moment more to remember I was there, but with a sigh he put the object down again. "Thank you, Dennison," he said. "You will call me if you find anything else, won't you? Yes, yes. Now Varig will show you out."

He must have pressed a button, because immediately the servant was at the door. Hoogstraten did not say good-bye.

That night I dreamed of her, a dream which Tennyson might have written for me, or one of the Cavalier poets, and I had a hard time explaining my abstraction to the sweet girl I was going with. *She* was in my mind, and would not leave, and I began to hope I'd never find another object for her husband, no matter how profitable the find might be.

As it turned out, during the next several months I found three things that seemed to have been made especially for him, and on each occasion he demanded that I bring them to him in New York. I justified it by telling myself that, after all, I was a dealer and could not forego such easy money, but I know now that it was far more the hope of seeing her even for a moment, of hearing her speak a few casual words. I dreamed of her time and again, and tormented myself with the thought of her embraced in her husband's coldness.

My second visit went much like the first, except that she was in the room when I arrived, again attired very simply in—but what she wore is of no moment. She stood up when I walked into her presence, and though again Hoogstraten did not introduce us, she thanked me for the machine—was it not a machine?—I had sold Andreas, which had pleased him. He was a genius. His mind, it demanded problems... It was very nice of...

I stood there tongue-tied, trapped by the magic radiating from her. Hoogstraten was already opening what I had brought him—a clock but not a clock. A thing with complicated clockwork in a case which could have been made by some exotic Fabergé, which told something, but not time—at least not any time that might make sense to us. After a moment, his voice still soft, he told her to leave the room, and without demur, as I stood there grinning at her foolishly, she left. For that I hated him, and almost for spite I asked him seven thousand for the thing. He paid me seventy-five hundred, again in cash, and sent me on my way.

Two months passed before I went again, two months during which I still dreamed of her, still thought of her, wondered at whatever power she had over me, at what her life might have been before she married Hoogstraten and, indeed, why she had married him.

This time, again, she was in the room when I arrived, and again she spoke to me, nothing memorable, comments about the season possibly, or how very good I was to find another treasure for Andreas. Then, once more, he sent her out; and the performance was repeated.

He first became wholly absorbed in what I'd brought—what was it? Half book, half Byzantine icon?—but written in a script completely alien to me, resembling none I'd seen before, which seemed to change as its pages turned, momentarily revealing illustrations that vanished almost instantly. He was delighted with it, and paid me far more than I would have dared to ask. Then, for the first time, he became almost friendly.

"Dennison," he said, "where do these come from? Why were they made? Was it simply as a challenge to me, to my intellect? I have no doubt that some of them came from hidden cultures, arts not permitted to the masses, lost civilizations, perhaps even other worlds! But *why*? Again, I ask you, is it deliberate? A continuing contest? To see if I, Andreas Hoogstraten, have a breaking point?" He stood. From a skeletal cabinet as convoluted as the last agony of an El Greco saint, he lifted a vessel, which I had seen before, but which I had taken simply for some far-out potter's drug-dream. He handed it to me. Perhaps a foot high, almost opaque, it was enormously heavy.

"Look at it, Dennison," he said. "Do you know what it is?"

Up close, it looked like grayish glass, but with a higher lustre, and it was much, much heavier. Like any vase, it tapered to a neck, but there the resemblance ceased, for the neck doubled back on itself to penetrate the body halfway down and emerge again in a mouth melding with the other side.

"It is a Klein bottle, Dennison. Are you familiar with the Moebius Strip?"

Unknown Things

"You mean a strip of paper you give a sort of twist to and then join its ends so that in effect it has one side only?"

"Exactly. Well, a Klein bottle is like that, only in three dimensions. Its inside is its outside and vice versa. Do you understand?"

I said I understood.

He took it from me, looked at it with an expression of mixed pride and anger. "I have drilled into it, Dennison. I have used a little instrument with which surgeons look into our bodies' inmost secrets. Inside it is a complex of beautifully ground crystals, and what seem to be controls and things I cannot put a name to. So far, it is the only unknown thing that has defeated me. I have had it several years, and I know no more about it than when it came to me, but my getting it could not have been an accident. It was part of the test, the challenge."

Shocked at his megalomania, I fumbled for something innocuous to say. "I—I suppose you have a pretty large collection by this time, Mr. Hoogstraten?"

He replaced the Klein bottle in the cabinet. "A large collection?" He said it with a sneer. "Dennison, I have always two or perhaps three. They do not defeat me for very long. Indeed, this is the only one I have had to keep for several years."

"But what do you do with them?" I asked. "Do you give them away or sell them?"

"Certainly not. When I have solved them, when they have served their purpose, I destroy them. That is the only way for me perhaps to get revenge, you understand?"

Frankly, I was horrified. I protested that some of them were treasures, that they exhibited superb craftsmanship, that scientists would be interested in them.

He cut me off. "Never!" he cried. "When I have solved them, they are nothing! *Nothing!* They no longer have a soul!"

He paid me even more than he had previously, and exacted a promise that I'd keep hunting for him; and I left telling myself that no matter what I found, I'd never go back again.

It was five months before I did, just after I returned from my annual trip to England, and then it was because I knew I had to see her one more time. In a sense, she had never left me. I would wake at night from my Pre-Raphaelite dreams of her, despairing, wondering how ever she could have married him—not for his money, certainly. But why, why, *why*?

So I went back. The thing I'd found was simple—a crude tool, mysterious only in the fact that it had no discernible function. This time, when the man-servant admitted me, I saw that she wasn't in the room, and all the while Hoogstraten examined what I'd brought him, I kept looking at the door through which she had come and gone, wishing, hoping.

Finally he rose. "I will take the tool," he told me, "even though it is not of so high a quality. I shall pay four hundred only."

I could control myself no longer. "I haven't seen Mrs. Hoogstraten," I said, I hoped casually.

He stopped counting money. For moments, those cold, glistening pupils stared at me. Then, "No," he said, ever so gently. "You see—" he smiled, "—I found out what she was."

4
Bug-Getter

Although this is one of Bretnor's shortest stories, it has many of the characteristics that distinguish his style: a sense of humor, an efficient use of well-chosen words, and a science fiction element which is closer to fantasy than to science. "Bug-Getter" was first published in The Magazine of Fantasy & Science Fiction *in 1960. It was also included in* 100 Great Science Fiction Short Stories, *edited by Isaac Asimov, et. al., published by Doubleday & Co. in 1978, and* Laughing Space: Funny Science Fiction Chuckled Over, *edited by Isaac Asimov, et. al., and published by Houghton Mifflin Co. in 1982.*

Ambrosius Goshawk was a starving artist. He couldn't afford to starve decently in a garret in Montmartre or Greenwich Village. He lived in a cold, smoke-stained flat in downtown Pittsburg, furnished with enormously hairy overstuffed objects which always seemed moist, and filled with unsalable paintings. The paintings were all in a style strongly reminiscent of Rembrandt, but with far more than his technical competence. They were absurdly representational.

Goshawk's wife had abandoned him, moving in with a dealer who merchandized thousands of Klee and Mondrian reproductions at $1.98 each. Her note had been scrawled on the back of a nasty demand from his dentist's collection agency. Two shoddy subpoenas lay on the floor next to his landlord's eviction notice. In the litter, unshaven and haggard, sat Ambrosius Goshawk. His left hand held a newspaper clipping, a disquisition on his work by one J. Herman Lort, the nation's foremost authority on Art. His right hand held a palette-knife with which he was desperately scraping little green crickets from the unfinished painting on his easel, a nude for which Mrs. Goshawk had posed.

The apartment was full of little green crickets. So, for that matter, was the Eastern half of the country. But Ambrosius Goshawk was not concerned with them as a plague. They were simply an intensely personal, utterly shattering Last Straw — and, as he scraped, he was thinking the strongest thoughts he had ever thought in his life.

He had been thinking them for some hours, and they had, of course, travelled far out into the inhabited Universe. That was why, at three minutes past two in the afternoon, there was a whir at the window, a click as it was pushed open from the outside, and a thud as a small bucket-shaped spaceship landed on the unpaid-for carpet. It opened, and a gnarled, undersized being stepped out.

"Well," he said, with what might have been a slightly curdled Bulgarian accent, "here I am."

Ambrosius Goshawk flipped a cricket over his shoulder, glared, and said, "No, I will NOT take you to my leader," decisively. Then he started working on another cricket who had his feet stuck on a particularly intimate part of Mrs. Goshawk's anatomy.

"I am not interested with your leader," replied the being, unstrapping a super-gadgety spray-gun. "You have thought for me, because you are wanting an exter-

Bug-Getter

mination. I am the Exterminator. Johnny-with-the-spot, that is me. Pronounce me your troubles."

Ambrosius Goshawk put down his palette-knife. "What won't I think of next?" he exclaimed. "Little man, because of the manner of your arrival, I will take you quite seriously. Seat yourself."

Then, starting with his failure to get a scholarship back in art school, he worked down through his landlord, his dentist, his wife, to the clipping by J. Herman Lort, from which he read the following passage:

> ...and it is in the work of these pseudo-creative people, of self-styled "artists" like Ambrosius Goshawk, whose clumsily crafted imitations of photography must be a thorn in the flesh of every truly sensitive and creative critical mind, that the perceptive collector will realize the deeply-researched validity of the doctrine I have explained in my book *The Creative Critical Intellect* — that true Art can be "created" only by such an intellect when adequately trained in an appropriately staffed institution, "created," needless to say, out of the vast treasury of natural and accidental-type forms — out of driftwood and bird-droppings, out of torn-up roots and cracked rocks — and that all the rest is a snare and a delusion, nay! an outright fraud.

Ambrosius Goshawk threw the clipping down. "You'd think," he cried out, "that mortal man could stand no more. And now" — he pointed at the invading insects — "now there's this!"

"So," asked the being, "what is this?"

Ambrosius Goshawk took a deep breath, counted to seven, and screamed, "CRICKETS!" hysterically.

"It is simple," said the being. "I will exterminate. My fee—"

"Fee?" Goshawk interrupted him bitterly. "How can I pay a fee?"

"My fee will be paintings. Six you will give. In advance. Then I exterminate. After, it is one dozens more."

The Timeless Tales of Reginald Bretnor

Goshawk decided that other worlds must have wealthy eccentrics. He watched while the Exterminator put six small paintings aboard, and he waved a dizzy good-bye as the spaceship took off. Then he went back to prying the crickets off Mrs. Goshawk.

The Exterminator returned two years later. However, his spaceship did not have to come in through the window. It simply sailed down past the towers of Ambrosius Goshawk's Florida castle into a fountained courtyard patterned after somewhat simpler ones in the Taj Mahal, and landed among a score of young women whose figures and costumes suggested a handsomely modernized Moslem heaven. Some were splashing raw in the fountains. Some were lounging around Goshawk's easel, hoping he might try to seduce them. Two were standing by with swatters, alert for the little green crickets which occasionally happened along.
The Exterminator did not notice Goshawk's curt nod. "How hard to have find you," he chuckled, "ha-ha! Half-miles from north, I see some big palaces, ha, so! All marbles. From the south, even bigger, one Japanese castles. Who has built?"
Goshawk rudely replied that the palaces belonged to several composers, sculptors, and writers, that the Japanese castle was the whim of an elderly poetess, and that the Exterminator would have to excuse him because he was busy.
The Exterminator paid no attention. "See how has changing, your world," he exclaimed, rubbing his hands. "All artists have many success. With yachts, with Rolls-Royces, with minks, diamonds, many round ladies. Now I take twelve more paintings."

Bug-Getter

"Beat it," snarled Goshawk, "You'll get no more paintings from me!"

The Exterminator was taken aback. "You are having not happy?" he asked. "You have not liking all this? I have done job like my promise. You must paying one dozens more picture."

A cricket hopped onto the nude on which Goshawk was working. He threw his brush to the ground. "I'll pay you nothing!" he shouted. "Why, you fake, you did nothing at all! ANY good artist can succeed nowadays, but it's no thanks to YOU! LOOK AT 'EM — there are as many of these damned crickets as ever!"

The Exterminator's jaw dropped in astonishment. For a moment, he goggled at Goshawk.

Then, "CRICKETS?" he croaked. "My God! I thought you said 'CRITICS!'"

5
Aunt's Flight

Aunt's Flight was originally published in The Magazine of Fantasy & Science Fiction, *July, 1988.*

Charles Augustus Lindbergh was the first man to fly alone across the Atlantic — there's no doubt about that — but he was not the first *person* to do so. That honor — and I believe we can all agree it was an honor — belongs to my great-aunt, Miss Trivia Lacklustre of Goose Falls, Massachusetts, where the Lacklustre side of our family has lived since the Seventeenth Century.

She was a big, tall, gaunt woman with bright little black eyes in her pale face and her hair done in a great flat brown bun on the top of her head. (My father always insisted it wasn't real hair at all but a specially large cow-flop she'd picked up someplace. But then he never did like her.) Anyhow, she'd inherited the old Lacklustre place, which she ran well enough, farming it with the help of a couple of hired men, and taking an active part in the doings of the Goose Falls Congregational Church, where everyone said she was sweet on old Mr. Barrow, the widowed pastor, who paid her no heed at all. Anything needed doing around the church or in the congregation, or for that matter in all of Goose Falls, what there was of it, she pitched in and did, elbowing aside anybody who got in her way. But the folks put up with it

Aunt's Flight

because she could always be counted on to help with the kids or take care of granny or bake a half-dozen big apple pies or come over quick if a sheep or something needed help birthing.

Goose Falls didn't exactly love Aunt Trivia, but they sure didn't hate her. One thing especially they *didn't* like was her doing all her shopping at Monkey Ward's down to Salem instead of at Luke Correy's general store. It seemed like she thought Goose Falls wasn't good enough for her. (Of course, everybody else shopped at Monkey Ward's too, but that was only once in a while. Remember, this was back in 1904, before the Wright Brothers had got off the ground at Kitty Hawk even, and she had to get her big bay horse harnessed up to the buckboard each time and drive clear over there, all of six miles.) Anyway, she did it, and it was there she bought all her brooms — *all* of them, because she went through brooms like old Sherman going through Georgia. Every time she took over from anybody, first thing she did was fetch her own broom and sweep the place out, sweeping like crazy. Didn't matter was it the church or the Odd Fellows hall or the grocery store post office corner.

Anyhow, every time she'd wear a broom out, she'd get mad as anything and hurry over to Monkey Ward's to raise hell about it. She wouldn't speak to anyone except the manager of the Housewares Department, Junius Brutus Badger himself — a thin, sour man with gray sidewhiskers and a tight mouth, who always wore a heavy gold watch-chain with a funny green stone charm hung to it. The gossip was his family had been in Salem when the first Pilgrims got there, which made him a part Indian, I reckon. Mostly, folks were scared of him because he was so formal and cold, sort of like you'd expect of an undertaker. But not Great-aunt Trivia. No, sir!

That summer, when she'd wore out a brand new broom in just one busy weekend, first thing Monday morning she brought it in, waving it under Junius Brutus' nose like it was something dirty the cat'd done.

"Look at this, Badger!" she cried. "Monkey Ward's ought to be ashamed, they should, selling such trash! Why, I —"

Mr. Badger interrupted her. "*Montgomery* Ward's," he declared frigidly. "*Montgomery* Ward's, Mrs. Lacklustre."

Miss Lacklustre!" she shot back.

Well, it was sort of a standoff. There they were, looking each other right in the eye, and she told me it was like his thinking engine was going eighty to the dozen, while she kept on waving that broom so the whole store could see it. It must've lasted two-three minutes, but finally he actually smiled, just a little, like a one-inch crack in an iceberg, but something she'd never seen him do before.

"Mrs. Lacklustre," he said, "You are an established customer — may I say a valued customer? — of *Montgomery* Ward's. So —" He cleared his throat, and it sounded like something dry rubbing its hind legs together. "—so I shall bring you a new broom with our compliments. It is a very special broom, of an advanced design, and it will not only stand up to any usage you may put it to, but will also ease your labors."

"I'm not asking to ease up my labors!" sniffed Aunt Trivia, indignant that anybody'd think such a thing.

"I shall have to go home to get it," he continued, "for my family has been giving it its first trial, so I must

Aunt's Flight

ask you to wait — oh, perhaps fifteen minutes. If you'd care to go back to my office, I shall have one of the clerks prepare tea for you."

She didn't answer him, but sat down, managing to convey the idea that she'd never accept tea from anyone who sold brooms that wore out before you could even get the school house swept out. While she waited, she voiced her complaints to every customer who came within range, and when Junius Brutus returned she was feeling quite a bit better.

She regarded the broom he was carrying, and remarked she'd never seen the like of it in her born days, and wasn't it too big to get into corners? and what kind of straw was it made of, all funny and foreign looking? and that sort of silvery wire it was bound to the stick with?

Dubiously, she took it in hand. "Why, it hardly weighs *anything*!" she exclaimed, taking a couple of test swipes at the carpet.

His hand on her elbow, Junius Brutus started escorting her to the door. "I can promise you that as your workday advances it'll weigh less and less if you want it to. You'll find it a most versatile broom, Mrs. Lacklustre — a true scientific triumph. And you're the first to have one anywhere in these parts, at least nowadays — I mean before they come on the market, as it were. You'll find it *responding* to you, Mrs. Lacklustre, so you mustn't—" To her amazement, he actually winked at her. "—let too many people know about it. For business reasons, that is, yes indeed. No, don't thank me. Thank *Montgomery Ward's*."

The Timeless Tales of Reginald Bretnor

He walked her clear to the buckboard, and helped her up into it, and it seemed to her that the broom in her hand was also giving her a help up.

"Well, it better last longer than the last one you sold me," she said ungraciously as she gathered the reins.

"Oh, it will, it will!" Junius Brutus Badger assured her.

As I may have suggested, Aunt Trivia was a woman of great strength of character, and when she began to find out what her new broom really could do, it didn't faze her one bit. She started right off by sweeping her kitchen, and right in the middle of it the egg man knocked at the door. "Well," she said to the broom, like one talks to things when one's alone. "You just stand there till I see who's here. I'll be back in two shakes."

Without looking she went to lean it back in a corner, got her eggs, said good-bye to the egg man, and turned back to it. It wasn't leaning against the wall. Broom end up, it was standing straight up on its end, waiting for her.

"Sakes alive!" she exclaimed, mightily pleased. "Why, I bet you could fly clear up to the ceiling had you a mind to!"

Slowly, the broom rose till its straws touched the ceiling, where it brought down a cobweb she'd not seen before.

"Why, it's just like those books by Mr. Jules Verne!" she thought; and after that there was nothing for it but she had to experiment. It didn't take her more'n half a day to find out the broom could not only fly by itself, but also carry anything she put on it, including herself.

Aunt's Flight

"It'll be just the thing to take little rides on in the cool of the evening," she thought, "specially if I fix me some sort of sidesaddle. I'm sure not going to try straddling a hard, narrow thing like that broom handle. Besides, it wouldn't be modest."

She got to work and fixed up a sort of sidesaddle out of an old leather seat cushion, with a clamp to fasten it on with, but so she could take it off in no time when she had sweeping to do; and she started taking short flights after nightfall, first making sure the hired hands wouldn't catch on. She knew about the old days in Salem, and what they did to women they suspected of broom-riding and such, and she didn't want anyone getting ideas even though she knew her broom was some kind of new French invention.

I was probably the only person she told the whole story to. She was pushing eighty at the time, and I was only a little squirt, but I was her favorite grandnephew, and she knew I wasn't one to go gossiping round. She told me how she stitched a stirrup to that saddle, and fastened a sort of horn to it like regular ladies' saddles used to have for her other leg. It was then, too, that she suddenly got suspicious of Junius Brutus' intentions. *I'll just bet*, she told herself, *old Badger's figuring on me getting interested and flying way up high and maybe a big wind hitting me and my falling off. That'd get me out of his hair, wouldn't it just!* That was when she invented the first safety belt, something she should've gotten a patent on, making it out of the cinch from her daddy's old Whitman saddle. "With that round me, I was safe as houses," she told me. "Why, I could even doze off and sleep like a baby, my head resting on the straw part."

The Timeless Tales of Reginald Bretnor

On those first flights, she just went up a few hundred feet so she could look down on Goose Falls and parts of Salem, simply enjoying the air, and maybe dipping down once in a while to peek into somebody's window. But after two-three weeks of that she found it no longer satisfied her. She remembered she'd never really been much of anywhere, excepting that one trip to Atlantic City her folks took her on when she turned twenty-one, when the seagull spoiled her best Easter hat. And she began to wonder about all sorts of places she'd read about, like New London and Boston and William Penn's Philadelphia. And the more she wondered, the further away she wanted to go.

She dreamed about flying to Richmond, and getting there a sight faster than Daddy had when he was soldiering, and visiting New Orleans, though she'd heard it was wicked. But even that wasn't enough. Finally she realized that it was to England she really wanted to go, where her ancestors came from and which her granny always kept talking about even though she'd never been there. So she made her decision. She'd fly over to England and then maybe to France, but she'd tell folks she was going up to visit her second cousin, Braddock Lacklustre, up in Halifax, Nova Scotia. He was from the Tory side of the family, who'd moved north when General Washington won, but still he'd be happy to see her, if he and his sons weren't out after herring.

She planned everything very carefully. She got out her daddy's old, black Civil War saddlebags, and her Iver Johnson revolver in case of eagles and such, and a big, light wicker suitcase in which she could stash her saddle and stuff whenever she landed, and her ma's big rabbit-skin coat in case it got cold; and she made up a

Aunt's Flight

slew of sandwiches for the trip over, and bought herself a new thermos from Monkey Ward's for her coffee. She figured she could always get water. Some of the most important things, like a little compass in a gold-plated locket and her geography book with maps from back in her grammar school days, and a new Monkey Ward catalogue in case she had to tend to the wants of nature, she added in last.

That very night she took off. There was a real harvest moon up, and a lovely soft breeze, and after she got to maybe a thousand feet up she just gave the broom its head and followed the coastline, glorying in the moon's light on the sea and singing old favorites to herself: The *Lost Chord,* and *John Brown's Body,* and *Kiss Me Again, Nellie* and suchlike.

After a bit, she started taking an occasional nap; and she reached Halifax just before daybreak fresh as a daisy. She landed out of sight behind some trees on a hillside, hid all her gear in the suitcase after treating herself to some coffee, and walked on into town.

The very first person she met, an old milkman, told her exactly where Cousin Braddock was living and very kindly gave her a ride almost all the way there; and Cousin Braddock's wife and daughters were right glad to see her, even though he was off fishing and she'd woken them up. She stayed with them a couple of days, hoping he'd be back, but they guessed the herring must really be running, so finally she bade them good-bye, first sweeping out their whole house and their barn so she wouldn't be too beholden to them.

She knew that, so long as she took off in the dark and kept high enough, it wouldn't really matter whether she flew day or night, so she left before sunrise and headed for Iceland, which her geography book seemed to show as the best place to set down. She was really enjoying herself, watching the fishing boats and big ships down on the ocean, and after a bit she ate a couple of her sandwiches and one of the two kipper herrings Braddock's wife had wrapped up for her; it seemed like no time at all before she found herself over Iceland, only she could hardly believe it because there was no ice at all.

She dropped down at dusk right near a big log farmhouse; then, carrying her broom and her suitcase, she knocked at the door, meanwhile petting the big dog that came out barking at her. Well, the farmer and his family couldn't speak English, and she didn't know a word of their language, but she counted up to ten for them in Norwegian, and they laughed and invited her in, just in time to set down to dinner.

Next morning, before she said good-bye to them, she swept out, not just their house, but also their barnyard, which they sure appreciated. (The broom straws looked as if they were wearing a bit, but she decided she'd not worry about it just then.)

The weather was still wonderful, but the breeze was a lot stiffer, so she had to tie down her old Waster hat with a scarf. After a bit, she began to get bored, and so once, just for fun, she swooped down on a rusty old freighter and called out hello to the crew who looked like they were maybe Portygees or Greeks. Then she felt sort of sorry, because didn't they take on! They ran back and forth, shouting and making all sorts of strange signs, and one or two of them actually jumped overboard. So she waved them good-bye, and flew on.

Aunt's Flight

She saw a few whales, but not one single iceberg, and no birds of prey menaced her, so she ate her lunch and settled down for a nap. No one was watching the skies back in those days — in fine weather there was no need to. There were no aircraft out patrolling, and no ack-ack guns to go shooting you down. The eagles and hawks she'd halfway expected never did show up, but of course there were seagulls. When she woke up, she spied one of them following her, flying right below her, no more than a couple of yards off. Then she remembered what had happened to her hat back in Atlantic City—and right then nature called.

Abruptly, she got an idea. She whispered to her broom to fly really carefully, and she waited till that old gull was directly in line. Then she let go—and scored a direct hit, right amidships—*thwack*! "It maybe wasn't too ladylike," she told me, "but it sure did my heart good, paying him back for my hat."

She spent the next night in Ireland, but far up in the hills because she didn't know anyone there, and because she'd heard things about the Irish in Boston. Then she flew off to England with the highest of hopes, only to have them shattered almost immediately. Most of all, she'd wanted to see London, but when she looked down all she could see was coal-smoke, and that in midsummer. It was the same over Birmingham and about ten other cities.

Of course, she could've set down someplace in the country, but she was so annoyed after all her trouble and having come all that way that she sat back on her saddle and actually wondered whether she ought to fly straight home again. Then she remembered a school teacher who was a friend of her daddy's and who was always talking about the south of France, about Nice and those places, and how wonderful it was there.

"Well," she said to herself, "why not?"

She looked up the south of France in her geography book, consulted her compass, and set off directly; and before very long she found herself looking down on the blue, blue Mediterranean and on Nice itself. She checked against her map to make sure, and that's what it was, so she circled it several times, looking for a likely landing spot. The air was warm, and the land smelled just lovely, and she told herself that if she swooped down fast enough and lit maybe in a wood, chances were either nobody'd see her or even if they did it wouldn't matter too much — after all, it wouldn't be like being seen by people back home.

The truth of the matter was that all the color and the softness of the breeze and the sweetness of the smells were getting to her, and later on she realized that probably it was just as foolish to come down in broad daylight in France as anywhere, but I guess she was plain lucky. She swooped down as fast as she could behind a low hill, and around it, and suddenly she found herself in a neat little wood, standing on a carpet of grass with flowers growing at her feet. Quick as could be, she unlimbered and got things stowed away in her suitcase. Then she walked into the wood, into sunlight beaming down and golden shadows. She walked for maybe five minutes, listening to the birds singing — and the wood abruptly came to an end.

She found herself in a park, a miniature park, but one as carefully tended as if it surrounded a palace. There was a small marble fountain splashing a few yards away. There was beautifully manicured green grass, and beds

Aunt's Flight

of irises and roses and little forget-me-nots and any number of other flowers. Across the park rose a miniature castle, a pocket-size palace. And only a few feet from where she stood, at a fine linen tablecloth spread on the grass, a bearded elderly gentleman had been pouring champagne into a young lady's glass. His arm was round her waist, which would have been tiny even without the corset holding the rest of her, which wasn't tiny at all.

"*Oooh!*" gasped Aunt Trivia, recognizing him from his photograph.

He stopped pouring. He stared at her. He frowned. "My good woman, what are you doing here?" he demanded in French. "Don't you know you're trespassing?"

"Ooooh!" Aunt Trivia repeated. "I — I know who you are, sir, Your Majesty, I reckon it is. You're King Edward, only I've forgotten your number. I — I didn't mean to butt in, but I just flew over from Massachusetts — that's in the U.S. of America — and I — well, I —"

The young woman laughed lightly. "Did you hear her, Bertie? She just *flew* over, and she's one of my countrywomen. Do you suppose she flew on that broom?"

Aunt Trivia had seen the young lady's picture too, but she couldn't remember her name though she recalled her being on the stage or something like that and not properly what they'd have called a lady back home.

"Yes, ma'am," she answered. "That's true. I did fly on my broom. I wouldn't of set down here if I'd known about you folks. But I was getting mighty hungry, and everything was so pretty, and the air smelled so good, I figured I just wouldn't wait. Just so you'll know who I am, my name's Trivia Lacklustre, and I'm from Goose Falls."

The king chuckled. "Did you say *Trivia*? Isn't that a rather unusual name?"

"Yes sir. Everybody in my family thinks it must've been short for something, but none of 'em can remember just what."

He turned to the lady. "Well, Lily," he said, "what do we do about her? Shall we call the servants and have her chucked out?"

Lily patted his hand. "Oh, let's not do that. After all, I know she's telling the truth about being American — she's a real Down East Yankee — no matter how she really did get here. You heard her say she's hungry. Why not tell her to put down her broom and that suitcase and join us? There's lots left, and I'd love to hear her story."

"Lily, I can deny you nothing," laughed Edward VII. "Miss Trivia, will you join us?"

Aunt Trivia allowed as she'd be happy to, and she put her stuff down and took off her hat; and she was surprised to see that the king's face, when he looked at her hair, had exactly the same expression as my old man's used to have. But he himself seated her on the grass. Then he waved away two large Frenchmen who came looming up, and served her a small roasted fowl, which she found delicious, and some caviar, which she ate out of politeness; and while she ate they listened to her story, pouring more champagne for her every time her glass emptied.

She told them everything, all about buying her broom from Junius Brutus at Monkey Ward's, and how he'd sworn it'd never wear out, but that it was getting sort of ragged even though she'd hardly used it at all,

Aunt's Flight

and about Iceland and how she'd swooped down on the freighter. All she left out was the seagull. She got to feeling more and more at home with them as the champagne took effect, and finally, quelling a small burp, she said, "You know, Your Majesty sir, back home we don't hold much with kings, except a few of us who headed up north to Canada when we won, but if we'd had a kind like you, Your Majesty sir, I guess maybe we'd still have one."

"That," said the king, "is indeed a pretty compliment, though I must say—" And he smiled at Miss Lily. "—I do seem to get along nicely with some of your compatriots."

Aunt Trivia said nothing, though she was pretty sure the lady was no better than she should be— but he was a king after all and they'd both treated her very kindly.

"And what do you plan to do now?" asked Lily.

"Well, I was sort of figuring on sweeping that castle of yours out for you, you feeding me that fine lunch and all."

They thanked her, but assured her it wouldn't be necessary because they had all sorts of servants to do it.

"Then I guess I'll just fly on home. There's no point to my staying away any longer. But you've shown me such a fine time I don't mind if you watch me take off." She started right in getting out her saddle and stuff, "Only — only you won't tell anyone, will you?"

"Hardly!" exclaimed the king. "I don't want to go down in history as Edward the Mad, like that poor Spanish Juana la Loca."

"Goodness gracious!" said Aunt Trivia. "We wouldn't want *that*!"

She got everything rigged up, tied the scarf good and tight over her hat, shook hands with Lily, did her best to curtsy before His Majesty, and took off straight into the air.

She said that when she turned round to wave back they were looking at her as if they couldn't believe their own eyes.

She flew straight on home, stopping only in Ireland and Iceland, and not even in Halifax, and the minute she'd unloaded she had the big bay hitched up and drove down to Salem.

She marched into Monkey Ward's Housewares Department waving her broom like a battle-ax, and right up to Junius Brutus Badger.

"Look at that, Badger!" she cried, pointing at the bent and broken ends of its straws. "You said it'd last me forever, you did. And you told me it was brand new." She held it under his nose and pointed at a tiny inscription on the stick just back of the wire binding: *Sufannah Badger*, it said, *1687*.

"Brand new!" she repeated, staring him right in the eye.

Junius Brutus Badger didn't argue. He gave her a new Monkey Ward broom out of stock and didn't charge her a dime.

So Aunt Trivia wasn't just the first person to fly the Atlantic all by herself; she was the first one to fly it both ways, and the first to fly it on a broom — and that's something no one else has done in all the years since then.

I guess they just aren't making brooms the way they used to.

6
Dr. Birdmouse

"Dr. Birdmouse" was first published in Fantastic Stories of Imagination, *April, 1962. Ten years later it was included in the Random House book* Strange Bedfellows: Sex and Science Fiction, *edited by Thomas Scortia. In 1987 it was published once again, this time in* Fantastic Stories: Tales of the Weird & Wondrous, *edited by Martin H. Greenberg and Patrick L. Price, a paperback from TSR, Inc.*

Dr. Birdmouse needed only two weeks to learn English. He met Vandercook every morning at the door of the spaceboat, and they walked — or, at least, Vandercook walked while Dr. Birdmouse flitted and fluttered — out over the crisp bluish grass into the pink trellis-trees, where they seated themselves on pillowy vegetables called thirmlings and throgs. Vandercook liked the throgs because they didn't squeak like the thirmlings, and besides they were dry.

Of course, it wasn't really as informal as that. Vandercook didn't actually walk *on* the grass, Dr. Birdmouse's odd little friends always unrolled a splendid red carpet that stretched from the door of the spaceboat through the out-grove, through the place where the gestures were made, into the in-grove. There they brought in the big breakfast banquet, a sort of fruit-salad-smorgasbord-vegetable-plate, and made their prettiest gestures as Vandercook ate it, keeping them up until Eetwee's twelfth moon — the quick, green one — made its third trip overhead.

Vandercook attributed all this to his own resourcefulness and quick thinking. As soon as Dr. Birdmouse had learned enough English to ask him his business, he had announced himself as Envoy Extraordinary and Ambassador Plenipotentiary from Earth to Eetwee. This ruse had made it unnecessary for him to tell Dr. Birdmouse the truth about his profession — how he travelled from planet to planet playing the piano, and how the light from the three romantic old curlicued oil-lamps shone on his slick wavy hair, and his spangled tuxedo, and his red smile and white, hairy hands — and how lean, lonely young women, and hungry middle-aged women, and wistful old women sat there and listened, devouring him with their moist, stupid eyes.

He had a bad moment or two when Dr. Birdmouse's personality, flowering with his fluency, began to bear an uncanny resemblance to that of his own Uncle Edwin, an elderly person of indeterminate sex with enough of an income to swish around on the edge of the Arts. After Dr. Birdmouse addressed him as "*dear* boy" several times, following this up with a perfect rendition of Uncle Edwin's soprano giggle, Vandercook asked him outright, "Are you reading my mind?" And Dr. Birdmouse giggled and swished, and replied, "*Dear* silly boy, I'd just *love* to read it and know *all* the sweet things you're thinking. But I can't. We're all awfully in*tui*tive here on dear little Eetwee, but I'm just not telepathic."

Vandercook settled down on his throg, fairly certain that the sweet things in his mind were safely concealed. These concerned what he had been doing before

Dr. Birdmouse

his arrival, and his plans for the future, which he had made within fifteen minutes after landing on Eetwee.

His profession was not as rewarding as it was said to have been back in the juicier days of the Twentieth Century, and he had been wanting to quit it. Besides, he was weary of ardent but unpleasing women, one at a time or by the whole hall full. He was sick and tired of the coarse jokes his fat brother, Hughie, was always cracking about them, especially in public and to his loud, red-faced friends. Hughie was a trucking contractor with a whole string of starlets and models and absolutely Grade-A nightclub strippers. Vandercook had been brooding about it. Suddenly he had made his decision, abandoned his manager-navigator, decamped with the spaceboat and proceeds. Then, promptly losing his way, he had blundered on Eetwee.

Well, pretty soon now, if he wanted, he'd be able to buy himself the world's fanciest harem. He imagined them — brunettes, blondes, and redheads, all in a sort of lush Turkish-bath setting, with Hughie drooling with envy outside the door. Boy, would that show him!

He had seen right away that Dr. Birdmouse's friends were worth money. They were worth so much money that even the spaceboat could carry enough of them to make him a fortune. Usually it wasn't worthwhile exhibiting extraterrestrials; they were too different. A couple of monkeys out of a zoo could steal their audience away any time. Besides, they required special atmospheres and temperatures, to say nothing of menus. But Dr. Birdmouse's friends were all oxygen breathers, and each of them looked so *almost* familiar that you could stare at it for hours just trying to figure it out. Then you'd finally conclude, as Vandercook had at first, that every one was a species all by itself.

Vandercook knew that if you take a tall glass, pour in a jigger of brandy and one of tequila, and then fill it up with champagne, you get something unique. It may remind you of what has gone into it, but it has new and special characteristics all its own, and they are decidedly functional. Dr. Birdmouse was like that. At first glance, he reminded Vandercook of the pouring together of a rather large bird, perhaps of the pheasant variety, and a very large mouse — not a forced crossing, not an unnatural linking of hostile genes, but a subtle blending which itself modified the ingredients. Dr. Birdmouse was not mouse *plus* bird. He rose above that. He had neither feathers nor fur, but he had their resultant, a soft covering which, beneath its gray surface, showed the bright patterns of his ancestral plumage. He had wings which folded discreetly so as not to mar his mousely appearance after he landed. He had a little, dark nose-beak which wiggled, hands fore and aft, and a parasol-fan at the end of his tail which he used as a stabilizer. He was Dr. Birdmouse, and nobody else. And in this single respect, of their utter uniqueness, all his friends were just like him.

As soon as he could, Vandercook had asked why this was. "Where is the rest of each species?" he asked. "Why is it I've seen only one of a kind?"

"Species? The rest?" Dr. Birdmouse looked startled.

"Sure," Vandercook said, "all the critters who're just like each other, all the bears or tigers or horses or owls, all the— well, all the birdmice."

Dr. Birdmouse

"You mean—" Dr. Birdmouse suddenly became very excited. "—you mean that you still have *species* on Earth?"

"Why, naturally," Vandercook answered.

"Gracious me! And— and they *aren't* interfertile?'

A great light burst on Vandercook. Taken a bit by surprise, he glanced quickly around at Dr. Birdmouse's friends, and gaped, and shook his head mutely.

"Dear me, dear me!" Dr. Birdmouse fluttered and swished, and jumped up and down on his thirmling. Then he calmed down a little, and patted Vandercook's knee. "You poor, *poor* creatures," he murmured. "How *dull* for you, dear boy."

After that, Dr. Birdmouse asked a great many questions; and Vandercook told him as much as he thought he could safely impart about reproduction on Earth, being very careful, of course, to avoid hurting his feelings.

When he had finished, Dr. Birdmouse did his best to console him. "You must try not to mind *very* much," he said gently, "because someday I'm sure you'll be civilized too. *We* were primitives once, before sweet Mr. Gibbon went into business. We had all *kinds* of species, reproducing themselves for no reason at *all*."

Vandercook asked him who sweet Mr. Gibbon had been, and Dr. Birdmouse immediately gestured at one of his friends, who handed over a heavy brown pouch he was carrying. From it, Dr. Birdmouse removed a fine three-dimensional likeness, cased in plastic, of what appeared to be a soberly spectacled, portly, striped ape with a vividly purple behind.

"Gibbon's as close as your language can come to his name," Dr. Birdmouse declared. "He accomplished all *sorts* of wonderful things, but the most marvelous of all were his medicines. The first one was called *Mr. Gibbon's Mental Invigorator,* and he sold it in the *dearest* little square blue bottles, and the other gibbons bought it *all* up, and they gave it to *every*one else to see what would happen. What happened, of course, was that pretty soon the gibbons weren't the *only* intelligent, civilized species any more, because all the rest were as clever as they were. The lions and tigers and things stopped killing and eating their new little friends, and became civil engi*nee*rs, and vio*li*nists, and in*sur*ance adjusters, and took Ph.D's in the most *in*teresting subjects. Everyone was *so* happy, dear boy."

For a moment, Vandercook toyed with the notion of getting a few hundred gallons of the Mental Invigorator, and giving it to the lions and tigers and things back on Earth, and, with their aid, taking over as dictator. Then he recalled that, on Eetwee, it had succeeded only in converting them all into pacifists, and he rather reluctantly went back to his more modest original plan.

"But they weren't *half* as happy as they were later *on,*" Dr. Birdmouse continued, "because it was then that *Mr. Gibbons's Genetic Catalyst* came on the market. It was flavored with *licorice,* and was *ever* so tasty, and it came in cute little square *green* bottles with a picture of dear Mr. Gibbon on the labels, so naturally everyone bought it. But the *best* thing about it was that it made all the species inter*fer*tile right then and there."

"*All?*" interrupted Vandercook, still slightly incredulous.

"All but the *fish*es, dear boy— and *they* wouldn't have been any fun. It works on the genes and the chromosomes and things so that they sort of *alter* each other, and adapt, and only the *love*liest characteristics show up,

Dr. Birdmouse

and everything works simply beautifully no matter *how* different we are. Nowadays, of course, the species are com*plete*ly mixed up, but still every new person who's born has what we call *dominants* — two of them, like bird/mouse, for example — and these keep us reminded of the bad, bad old days. It's all so ar*tis*tic! Here on Eetwee, dear boy, the *last* thing we'd do would be to separate the sheep from the goats. And it's here—" Dr. Birdmouse giggled and winked. "—that the lion *really* lies down with the lamb. Yes, *indeed*."

Vandercook began to see the full implications of Mr. Gibbon's design for living. Even he was appalled. "But that isn't possible!" he exclaimed. "I mean— after all— just the *mechanical* problems—"

Dr. Birdmouse assured him that there had been no problems at all. "Mr. Gibbon's Mental Invigorator made us all *very* clever," he said simply; and then, before Vandercook could pursue the subject, he dropped it with the promise that they'd go into details later. "But first, *dear* boy—" He beckoned to three of his friends, who came up, walking and slithering and hopping, and seated themselves. "—I want you to meet our young Mr. Snakepig— such a sweet, *sen*sitive person! He was shown in the National Academy, where he won a *first* prize. And this is Dr. Leopardsheep, who arranged him, and dear Miss Moosevulture— isn't she *splendid*? A remarkable specimen— who helped make the arrangement. She's Mrs. Leopardsheep now—"

Young Mr. Snakepig coiled his tail in embarrassment; Dr. Leopardsheep looked stolidly proud, and his consort quite monstrously coy. And Vandercook, looking at the arrangement, saw that, while snake/pig were clearly the dominants, it was possible to detect echoes and overtones of leopard/sheep here and moose/vulture there. He realized, too, that the art of genetic arrangement on Eetwee was like flower arrangement in Japan, only more so. He therefore politely remarked that Mr. Snakepig was a real masterpiece, that the geniuses who had conceived him deserved everyone's compliments, and that he was delighted to meet them.

Dr. Birdmouse repeated all this in translation, and his listeners were obviously pleased. The arrangement squirmed. The geniuses snickered and shuffled their feet. Then they all started talking at once.

"They're simply *charmed*, dear boy." Dr. Birdmouse declared, "and they're sure you've made all sorts of de*light*ful arrangements back on your own little planet, and they want you to tell them *just* how you did it, and how many *priz*es they won."

Most of Vandercook's brief affairs had been business transactions with well-heeled admirers who— he shuddered whenever he thought of it— invariably tried either to marry him or adopt him. Even when he had stayed around long enough to find out, there had never been any little arrangements. However, he slyly decided not to mention this to his listeners, and laid claim to some dozens of offspring. These, he boasted, had won all sorts of prizes, and it was on the tip of his tongue to declare that several of them had become Eagle Scouts, but he decided that the term might too easily be misinterpreted. All his children, he said, were handsome, healthy and normal. At this, Miss Moosevulture wanted to know what *normal* might mean; and, when Dr. Birdmouse informed her, she asked him to convey her sincerest condolences to their unfortunate visitor.

Dr. Birdmouse

Vandercook looked at the three of them, and pictured the customers drawn up in long, profitable lines in front of the box-office. These Eetweeans, he reflected, were smart cookies; there'd have to be a bit of lobotomy to take care of that...

Then he thanked Miss Moosevulture very courteously, and said that he was only too well aware of how dull life was on Earth, making the same old simple arrangements year after year. He explained that this was inevitable, because Man was superior to all the lower animals— present company excepted, of course. Still, he thought the two cultures could learn a great deal from each other; and that, he said, was why Earth had sent him to Eetwee— to invite an Eetweean cultural mission to return with him for a long, pleasant visit. He suggested that perhaps Dr. Birdmouse, and his three friends, and about eight or ten others would be about right for a starter.

Dr. Birdmouse seemed to have some difficulty translating his remarks, and the reason became obvious when he had finished. They all burst out laughing. Dr. Birdmouse hopped up and down. Young Mr. Snakepig coiled and squirmed. Dr. Leopardsheep and Miss Moosevulture rocked back and forth on their thirmlings.

"You dear, foolish, *sweet* boy!" Dr. Birdmouse gasped, when he had recovered enough to get a few words out. "Imagine us going to Earth! Whatever for? We have *so* much fun *here!*"

Vandercook controlled his impatience as well as he could. He spent a great deal of his time imagining how, in the midst of the ripest young women imaginable, he would be able to sneer, not only at Hughie and all his loud friends, but at his erstwhile patrons, plastered and dyed, ravenous, tearful, and wilted. These daydreams made him feel very masculine.

The rest of his time was devoted to long conversations with Dr. Birdmouse, and to keeping up with the Eetweean social swim— an expression which he only once had to take literally, when he was invited to dinner by an old Mr. Gullporpoise.

The conversations annoyed Dr. Birdmouse. He found Vandercook's descriptions of the life of an ambassador- plenipotentiary-and-envoy-extraordinary simply ridiculous. For the life of him, he said peevishly, he couldn't see how it left *any* time for artistic activities. It was completely un*n*atural.

And Vandercook answered that the reason it all seemed so strange to his host was that he was a man, not a birdmouse, and hadn't had the benefit of Mr. Gibbon's Mental Invigorator— and anyhow time was short, and he had to get home, and wouldn't Dr. Birdmouse and his friends please do Earth a big favor and agree to come with him?

Then Dr. Birdmouse would tell him all over again that there simply was no incentive, that they didn't want to learn about Ezra Pound's poetry, or nuclear fission, or *The Pines of Rome*, or even the comic book version of *Lady Chatterley's Lover*, because none of these, though probably worthy enough in themselves, had any bearings on making little arrangements.

Always, if Vandercook started to argue, it would be time for a banquet, or a gesture-parade; and Dr. Birdmouse would tell him never to mind, that it would all work out for the best because Eetwee was *really* the best of all possible worlds.

Dr. Birdmouse

What with frustrations like these, Vandercook's existence began to get pretty wearing. There were five banquets a day in the in-grove, and interminable rituals in the place where the gestures were made, and picnic-snacks in the out-grove between meals. There were visits to nearby cities, and leisurely strolls down their soft, latticed streets where, in the shade-squares, green spiders waved their slow fronds. And then there were tours of the art galleries and museums, which would have been more amusing if Dr. Birdmouse hadn't insisted on introducing him to all the exhibits, and forcing him, in his role of ambassador, to invent one banal compliment after another.

Vandercook taxed his ingenuity to the utmost to think up new arguments for a cultural mission, and got nowhere at all. Then, in the hope that the Mental Invigorator might sharpen him up, he began to hint more and more broadly that a shot of it would be welcome. His hints were ignored. Finally, during a party at Dr. Birdmouse's house, he located it in its little blue bottle on a shelf in the bathroom, right under the wall-tub, and swallowed it at a gulp. Next day he found himself able to fix a badly jammed zipper — a problem which had always defeated him in the past — with no trouble at all. Otherwise, it didn't seem to make any difference, and he felt quite discouraged.

He became irritable and impatient, and began to look haggard; and Dr. Birdmouse made it much worse by worrying about him. He took to fluttering sympathetically over his shoulder, regarding him oddly, and saying, "Are you *well*, dear boy? Are you sure you're perfectly *happy*? There aren't any bad little *troubles* you'd like to *tell* me about?"

For a while, getting desperate, Vandercook considered delivering an ultimatum: send the mission or be attacked by a space fleet with the most modern weapons. Something, however — perhaps Mr. Gibbon's Mental Invigorator — made him suspect that they would not be impressed. He settled instead on an ultimatum of a less violent nature.

"I'll be leaving this Tuesday," he casually told Dr. Birdmouse. "I hope that by then some of you decide to come with me. But whether you do or you don't, it's my turn to throw a party for *you* — just you, and President Bearpossum and his family, and a few intimate friends, Mr. Snakepig and his mother and father, you know. It'll be on my boat a few hours before I take off, and I'll serve mushrooms and artichoke hearts, and champagne, and those nice chocolate creams."

Naturally, he said nothing whatever about locking them into the hold and then pumping in a good, strong anesthetic; but Dr. Birdmouse went into a tizzy nevertheless. "Dear, *dear* boy!" he said shrilly. "You can't really *mean* that — not before we've even made up our *minds*. You've been *such* a problem; we've been thinking you *over*, and *talk*ing about you. And we do want to do the *right* thing, dear boy. We want to be sure you're *happy*. So please won't you *wait* a few days? I want you to have a long, cozy chat with Miss Cowturtle first. She's as *sweet* as can be, and she understands *all* these problems—"

After fifteen minutes of this, Vandercook agreed to have the chat with Miss Cowturtle, and said he'd defer his departure until Thursday evening. Beyond that he wouldn't give in.

"You've *changed*, dear boy," Dr. Birdmouse said sadly. "I don't suppose anyone gave you just a *wee*

Dr. Birdmouse

droppie of Mental Invigorator, did they? Darling Miss Moosevulture or someone like that?"

Vandercook chuckled, and told him about the episode in his bathroom, and apologized, and said he guessed he'd just been a bit thirsty.

And Dr. Birdmouse flicked the perspiration from his sharp little tongue, and said, "*Good*ness gracious! Imagine drinking that up *all* at once. And you *didn't* dissolve! I'm so relieved, dear boy."

For a few minutes, Vandercook felt decidedly shaken; apparently the unsupervised use of Mr. Gibbon's elixir had its perils. Then he manfully put such worries behind him, and concentrated on the carrying out of his plan. For the time being, this consisted of humoring the Eetweeans, and of keeping them as unsuspecting as possible.

He had a long, very dull chat with Miss Cowturtle. Dr. Birdmouse had taught her some English, and she asked Vandercook a great many questions in a dim, mooing voice, about his career, and if he felt really *adjusted*, and why Earth sent ambassadors out kiting around when they could have been much more useful making arrangements at home. He replied very cleverly, repeating his story with only slight variations; and he didn't allow himself to show any annoyance at Miss Cowturtle's unpleasant habit of retracting her horns and pulling her head back into her shell whenever she had to take notes. Whenever she did it, he simply thought of the starlets and models, and how jealous Hughie would be.

After that, he diplomatically accepted the President's invitation to spend his remaining few days with the Bearpossums in the Executive Mansion. He walked into the city with Dr. Birdmouse and young Mr. Snakepig. Though it lay even further from the groves than the spaceboat, the red carpets were spread every inch of the way, and even more Eetweeans were making gestures than usual. The four days that followed seemed endless. Sometimes he would corner the president, or one of the ministers, or Dr. Birdmouse himself, and ask whether they had reached a decision; and they always said they were ever so sorry, but they hadn't had time, and there was a banquet just starting next door, and wouldn't he like to come over?

Vandercook put on nine pounds. He was almost ready to burst when, after the third banquet on Thursday, President Bearpossum shook his hand at the door, and said how nice it had been to have him there as a house-guest — no trouble at all — and assured him that they'd all be delighted to come to any party he wanted to give, any time, and patted his back, and whispered that Dr. Birdmouse had something delightful to tell him about what they'd decided.

He was in very high spirits as he and the Doctor made their way back over the splendid red carpets. He stayed in high spirits even though the Doctor kept giggling and wouldn't tell him a thing except, "It's a *love*ly surprise — just too, too lovely for words."

They came to the in-grove, to the corner where the trellis-trees opened out on the clearing. "You *must* close your eyes, dear boy," Dr. Birdmouse declared. "That'll be *half* the fun."

Vandercook closed his eyes, expecting in a moment to see Dr. Birdmouse's friends — either as a cultural mission with their suitcases packed or as an eager little

Dr. Birdmouse

partying group. He didn't care which. Then Dr. Birdmouse led him around the corner and several feet forward. He opened his eyes—

"*There*!" Dr. Birdmouse exclaimed. "Isn't it *dar*ling? We've *built* you a *house*!"

Vandercook stared. The cultural mission was nowhere in sight. Before him he saw a round metal house like a very fat toadstool, with an outrigger porch and some round porthole windows. As Dr. Birdmouse guided him forward, he had a horrible feeling that somewhere he'd seen it before.

"Wh-where did you g-get it?" he gasped. "Th-that *metal*?"

"Out of your *nasty* old spaceboat," replied Dr. Birdmouse with pride. "We melted it down. We were sure you wouldn't *mind*, dear boy."

Vandercook followed him in through the door. He looked around at the spaceboat's tables and chairs, and at new pieces of furniture contrived from its once-working parts. He looked at his chrome-and-gold-plated piano, with the glamorous old-fashioned oil-lamps on it. Dr. Leopardsheep, Miss Moosevulture, and young Mr. Snakepig were all waiting there, wearing the self-satisfied expressions typical of welcoming committees.

"My G-God!" Vandercook croaked. "I— I'm *marooned*!"

"*Dear* boy," Dr. Birdmouse exclaimed. "How *clever* you are. You hit the sweet little nail right on the head!"

Everyone but Vandercook seemed tremendously pleased. All at once, the enormity of what had occurred burst on him. The light-years between Earth and Eetwee, instead of being just a short three-weeks hop, stretched out to their full awful length. The prospect of easy wealth derived from the sale of Dr. Birdmouse's friends vanished in cold, desolate darkness. So did the ladies who had been going to impress Hughie.

It was too much. Ranting and raving, Vandercook stamped up and down. Waving his plump, hirsute hands, he threatened the destruction of Eetwee and all its inhabitants. He used impolite terms to describe Dr. Birdmouse and all other Eetweeans, and spoke very unpleasantly about how superior Man was to the whole brute creation, of which, despite their intelligence, they were a part.

Dr. Birdmouse and his friends didn't interrupt him at all. Once, Dr. Birdmouse remarked, "*Poor* lad, he's de*lir*ious with joy," *sotto voce*; and Dr. Leopardsheep whispered something to his wife about "…sedatives?" But otherwise they said nothing until he ran down.

This happened quite suddenly. One moment he was getting all set to commit personal violence; the next, he had realized that, even though they were pacifists, Dr. Leopardsheep and Miss Moosevulture and young Mr. Snakepig were either horrifyingly fanged, impressively hoofed, or frighteningly muscled. He sat down abruptly.

Instantly, Miss Moosevulture came to him and began stroking his hand. Dr. Leopardsheep hemmed and hawed sympathetically. Dr. Birdmouse fluttered and swished, and said, "*Dear*, dear boy. It's *all* for the best. We've dis*cuss*ed and dis*cuss*ed you, and we're doing just the right thing."

He went on to explain that they had taken a liking to Vandercook the moment they saw him, but that for a long time they hadn't been sure whether they ought to keep him on Eetwee. They could tell that he was an art-

Dr. Birdmouse

ist at heart, and that he hadn't been happy moving around from world to world all the time — but still there was his career, and he seemed always so anxious to start off again. It was a real puzzle. The best minds on Eetwee had wrestled with it day and night.

"And you'll just *nev*er guess," Dr. Birdmouse said with a giggle, "what a *silly* thing I suggested at first. I thought that you *liked* diplomacy and skipping from planet to planet — just i*ma*gine! I should have guessed right away that you hated it all, and that you really wanted to settle down somewhere and make all sorts of *ducky* arrangements—"

The thought of ducky arrangements evoked a sharp mental picture. Vandercook shivered. "What do you know about it?" he said rudely. "Next you'll be telling me that you *can* read my mind!"

"Dear me, no," Dr. Birdmouse replied. "*I* can't— but Miss Cowturtle can. Bless her soul! Such a *nice* person. She was really quite good at it too, considering how strange it was to her. She caught several glimpses of some plans you were making. They were *awfully* romantic, but somehow you didn't seem to be really *too* happy about them. I mean, you didn't seem awfully *ar*dent. But she understood why with the first little peek: whoever it was you were thinking of seemed so *dowdy* and *plain*. And then— well, *then* she found out how badly you wanted to take some of us with you, and she got the feeling that you valued us *very* highly. We were *so* touched, dear boy. After that, President Bearpossum and Dr. Leopardsheep and young Mr. Snakepig and I all agreed that you were torn between love and duty, and that what you *really* wanted deep down inside was to stay here on dear little Eetwee—"

There was a small, timid knock on the door, and Dr. Birdmouse called out, "Come i-in," and Miss Cowturtle entered.

Vandercook regarded her with frank loathing. "You mean that thing read my mind?" he demanded. "That—that goddam cowturtle freak?"

"Oh, she isn't Miss Cowturtle any more," Dr. Birdmouse put in. "She's Mrs. Vandercook now."

"SHE'S *WHAT*?" Vandercook screamed.

"*Mrs.* Vandercook," Dr. Birdmouse repeated. "You can make your arrangements together. Won't that be *nice*?"

Vandercook looked around for an exit. There was only one, and Dr. Leopardsheep was showing his teeth right beside it. He thought of the old days, and the rows and rows of sweet, lean young women, and sweet, panting middle-aged women, and darling, wistful old women all eating him up with their lovely moist eyes. He burst into tears.

At once, Dr. Birdmouse and young Mr. Snakepig helped him into a chair. "You don't *have* to take on so, dear boy," said the Doctor. "I know it's wonderful, *won*derful news, but you mustn't let it affect you so *much*. After all, we did bring you to the honeymoon-groves *every* day, over the proper red *car*pets, and with all the best men and bridesmaids making their *love*liest gestures, and we did build your house right here in the *middle* to prepare you psychologically. We even saved your piano out for you. And now, dear boy" — he held out a small cordial — "just drink this and you'll feel *so* much better."

Blindly, Vandercook reached for the glass.

"Down the hatch," remarked young Mr. Snakepig.

Dr. Birdmouse

Vandercook swallowed it all, felt instantly better, and realized a little too late that it was flavored with licorice.

Miss Moosevulture clapped her wing-hands. "There!" she cried out delightedly. "I *told* you he wouldn't dissolve! I was sure all that was nonsense about Man being different from everyone else."

"I'm *so* glad," mooed Miss Cowturtle ardently.

"This is splendid," declared Dr. Leopardsheep. "For the first time in hundreds of years we have an entirely new species to work with. Mr. Vandercook, you will go down in history."

Vandercook saw the future in its full four dimensions — and found all of them utterly hideous. He showed the whites of his eyes, and pointed a palsied forefinger at Miss Cowturtle. *"No, no, n-n-no!"* he gibbered. "I c-c-can't be stuck here with *that!*"

Dr. Birdmouse laughed gently. "You won't be, dear boy. *We* understand you better than that. After all, this sweet person—" he bowed "—saw that your being an ambassador was just subli*mat*ion, and that you *really* wanted to spend the rest of your life flitting from one little mate to another like a *dear* little bee. Miss Cowturtle is just the *first* Mrs. Vandercook. Look out of the window."

Vandercook turned his head like a robot. Outside, at the door, they were patiently waiting— Miss Camelbat and Miss Hippogiraffe, Miss Goosemonkey and funny little Miss Frogterrier, Miss Yakpigeon and Miss Sealweasel and the fat, elderly Widow Horserabbit, and all their *nice* friends. The line ran from the door, through the place where the gestures were made, and the out-grove, all the way to the patch where the spaceboat had been.

Slowly, through his despair, Vandercook realized that they looked awfully familiar. Slowly, he began to feel strangely comforted.

He sobbed only once more. Then he went to the piano, and turned on his famous, soft smile, and — never taking his eyes from the ladies — began the *Moonlight Sonata*.

7
The Man On Top

Scott Alan Burgess in The Work of Reginald Bretnor: An Annotated Bibliography & Guide *(Borgo Press, 1989), writes that "The Man on Top" is "perhaps the author's best-known story." It is certainly one of his most widely republished works. Originally appearing in* Esquire *in Oct., 1951, it was also printed in* Senior Scholastic, The Magazine of Fantasy & Science Fiction, The 6th Annual Edition of the Year's Best Science Fiction, 14 Great Tales of ESP, 100 Great Science Fiction Short Stories, *and several other books and magazines in the U.S., Britain, Australia, Japan and Italy.*

Who was the first man to reach the summit of Mount Everest? Barbank, of course. Any school kid can tell you — *highest mountain in the world, 29,141 feet, conquered finally by Geoffrey Barbank.*

I was forgotten — I was just the fellow who went along. The press gave him the credit. He was the Man on Top, the Man on the Top of the World.

Only he wasn't, really. He knows that it's a lie. And that hurts — especially when he thinks of me, and of the Holy Man.

Jealous of Barbank? I don't think I am. And you won't either, presently.

I hated him. A mountain is a quest, a mystery, a challenge to the spirit. Mallory, who died on Everest, knew that — and his was the best reason for trying to climb it. "Because it is there," he said.

But Barbank climbed it to keep some other man from being first on top. He climbed it because he knew no other way of getting there. Mysteries did not exist for him, and anyone who felt the sense of mystery was a fool. All men were fools to Barbank — or enemies. They had to be.

I found that out the day I joined the expedition in Darjeeling. "The town's in a sweat about some flea-bag Holy Man," he told me after lunch. "Sort of a ten-goal saint, complete with extra supernatural powers. Let's go and look the old fraud over. Might have a bit of fun."

So the two of us walked down from the hotel, and, all the way, he boasted of his plans. I can still see his face, big, cold, rectangular, as he discussed the men who'd tried and failed—

Of course, they'd muffed it. You couldn't climb Everest on the cheap. *He'd* do things differently. All his equipment was better than the best. Because he had designed it. Because it cost a mint. Because—

It made me angry. But I had come too far to be turned back. I let him talk.

We turned into the compound of a temple. There was a quiet crowd there, squatting in the dust, and many monkeys. By a stone wall, under a huge umbrella, the Holy Man was seated on a woven mat. His long, white hair framed the strangest face I've ever seen — moon-round, unlined, perfectly symmetrical. His eyes were closed. Against the pale brown skin, his full lips curved upward like the horns of a Turkish bow. It was a statue's face, smiling a statue's smile, utterly serene.

The Man On Top

The people seemed waiting for something to begin. As we came through the crowd, it was so still. But Barbank paid no heed. We halted up in front. We stood there in the sun. And he talked on.

"What's more," he said, "I don't intend to bother with filthy Sherpa porters for the upper camps. Planes will drop the stuff. I'm making *sure* I'll be the man on top."

That set me off. "The Sherpa are brave men," I told him, "good mountaineers. Besides, it's more their mountain than it is ours."

"Rot," he snapped. "They're beasts of burden. There's nothing they can do that a machine can't do better. Natives are all the same." He pointed at the Holy Man. "Now, there's a sample for you. Look at that smirk. Pleased as punch with his own hocus-pocus — dirt, nakedness, and all. They've made no progress since the Year One."

The Holy Man was naked, or nearly so, but he was clean; his loincloth was spotless white. "Perhaps," I answered, "they're trying for something else?"

And slowly, then, the Holy Man looked up. He spoke to Barbank. "We are," he said.

I flushed, knowing that he had understood.

An instant later, I forgot embarrassment. I met his eyes — and suddenly the statue came alive. It was as though I had seen only the shell of his serenity, and now I saw its source. I felt that it was born, not in any rejection of the world, but in a knowledge of every human agony and joy — in a sophistication so complete that it was frightening.

"Yes, we are trying," the Holy Man went on. His voice was beautiful and strangely accented, and there was humor in it, and irony. "But for something else? I do not think so. It is just that we are trying differently, we of the East and West — and sometimes one cannot succeed without the other." Pausing, he measured Barbank with those eyes. "That is why I can help you, if you will only ask."

Barbank's mouth curled. "He's heard the gossip down in the bazaar," he said aside. "Well, he won't get a penny out of me."

The smile danced infinitesimally. "Must I explain? There is a thing you do not understand. A mountain is much more than rock and ice — especially if it is the highest in the world. No man can conquer such a mountain. His conquest can be only of himself."

I shivered. That was what Mallory had said.

"You damned old humbug!" Barbank's laugh roared out. "Are you trying to tell me that you can sit here on your dusty tail and help me reach the top?"

"I think I'd put it differently," the Holy Man replied. His fluid syllables were gently mocking now. "To be precise, I must say this. You never will achieve your heart's desire without my aid. Your way of doing things is not quite good enough."

Barbank's neck reddened. Fists clenched, he advanced a pace. Then he controlled himself. "Oh, isn't it?" he snarled. "Well, come along and watch! I can use one more mangy porter, I suppose. Damn you, you'll have a bird's-eye view!"

The Holy Man raised both his fragile hands. "Thank you — but no," he said; and his gentle irony cut with a fine, cruel edge. "I'd rather wait for you."

Barbank spat in the dust. He pivoted and strode off, pushing roughly through the murmuring crowd.

The Man On Top

It was then I decided that he must never be the Man on Top.

It is a long way from Darjeeling through Tibet to Chomo Lungma, the Mother Goddess of the Snows, which we call Everest. The journey takes some weeks.

We were eleven white men, but we soon found that we were not an expedition in the usual sense. We were Barbank's retainers, walled off by his contempt.

The others left him pretty much alone. I couldn't. The Holy Man's prediction was my obsession now. I took it as my cue, and laid my plans.

At every chance, I talked to Barbank about the mysteries of the peak — the awful Snow Men, whom the Tibetans all swear exist, and the dark, pulsating, flying things which Smythe had seen. I said that, very possibly, Mallory and Irvine had reached the summit first — that he might get to be the Man on Top only to find some evidence they'd left. I even suggested that the Sherps might have climbed it long ago. And always I shook my head, quoted the Holy Man, and told him he would fail.

When we reached our Base Camp on the Rongbuk Glacier, I was his enemy, who had to be defeated, cheapened, put to shame. And there was only one way to do that. Though Kenningshaw and Lane were better men, he chose me for the assault. I had to be there, to see the Man on Top with my own eyes.

And that was fine. Because I could only stop Barbank from being first on top by being there — by being first myself.

We followed the traditional approach — up the East Rongbuk Glacier and the East Wall of the North Col —

up to Camp Five, five miles above the sea. Below Camp Four, beyond which Barbank would not let them go, the porters gave him endless trouble — naturally. And, all the way, the mountain laughed at us. Against us, it sent its cruel light cavalry, the wind, the mist, the snow — harassing us, keeping us constantly aware of deadly forces held in close reserve.

Yet, when Barbank and I and Konningshaw and Lane stood at Camp Five and watched the plane from India trying to drop the final camp higher than any man had camped before, the sky was clear.

We watched the pilot try, and circle, and lose eight separate loads. And then the ninth remained; its grapples held.

"I bought two dozen, all identical," said Barbank. "I told you there's nothing these damn natives do that we can't do better." And we all hated him.

He and I reached Camp Six, at close to 28,000 feet, late the next afternoon. We set the tent up, and weighted it with its own cylinders of oxygen. Silently, we ate supper out of self-heating cans. We crawled into our sleeping bags. Restlessly fighting the subtle, dreadful cold, we finally slept.

We rose before the dawn, and found that the fine weather still held, and that there wasn't even a hint of the monsoon. We breakfasted. We drank our tea. We made ready to set off.

Barbank stood there, on the narrow ledge. He looked at the vast dark mountain, at the broad yellow band beneath the summit pyramid, at the depths of rock and glacial ice below. He looked at me.

"And so I won't succeed in my desire?" he taunted me. "*You bloody fool.*"

The Man On Top

Then he turned, and we went up. We mounted to the ridge, and stared down the awful precipice of the South Face, down, down, 15,000 feet to the Nepal hills. We worked our way toward the second step, where Mallory and Irvine were last seen. Though the great swords of the wind were sheathed that day, its small, keen lancets thrust through all our clothes down to our flowing blood. What snow there was was dazzling, the sky was an appalling blue, and the summit was a hidden thing behind its plume of cloud.

Toward that plume we worked. Even with oxygen, it was pure agony. Up there, the air is thin, thin, thin. The thinness of the air is in your flesh and bones, and in your brain. You move, and pause, and try to move again. And presently your whole attention is confined to that next move.

I can remember certain things. The sense of danger on the second step, the fear that it might prove unclimbable. Barbank stopping to rub the circulation back into his hands. The hiss of oxygen. My own raw throat. The rising wind. The skyline snow peaks off across Tibet.

On such a mountain, physically, there can be no question over who shall lead. But morally there can. I can remember husbanding my strength, giving Barbank a drudging minimum of aid, and waiting for my opportunity. I can remember Barbank weakening, relinquishing the lead high on a summit slab. I can remember the look in Barbank's eyes—

The hours had dragged. My watch had lied. Eight and nine, and ten. I moved. I ached. I forced myself to try and move again. Endlessly.

Then, without warning, the plume enfolded us. Now it was small, wind-shredded, tenuous. The Top of the World was 50 feet away.

I realized it. I knew that I would be the Man on Top, that I had Barbank where I wanted him. And suddenly I stopped. I don't know why. I laughed aloud. I waved him on. He passed by, hating me. I followed him.

He reached the summit edge. He turned his head. I could not see his lips, but I could feel their curl of triumph and their contempt. He turned again—

And, as he turned, a single gust screamed past us and laid the summit bare. I saw its rock. I saw a wide depression packed with snow.

But in the center there was no snow at all, for it had melted. On his woven mat, naked and serene, the Holy Man was waiting there.

Slowly, his moon-round face looked up. He smiled upon us with his statue's smile. His soft syllables flowed through the frozen air.

In that tone of pleased surprise with which one welcomes an unexpected guest, he spoke to Barbank. "*How* did you get up here?"

Barbank staggered. A strange sound came from his leather mask. Automatically, his arm came up and pointed — at the harsh summit, the ridge, the slabs, at all those miles of rock and ice and snow.

The Holy Man lifted both his hands. His gesture was exquisite, polite, incredulous. I could have sworn that in his voice there was no irony.

"You mean," he said, "you *walked*?"

8
The Beasts that Perish

"The Beasts that Perish" was first published in Ellery Queen's Mystery Magazine *in Dec., 1977, as "The Accident Epidemic." It was later included in the book* Ellery Queen's Scenes of the Crime, *edited by Ellery Queen, and published in hardcover by the Dial Press, Davis Publications, in 1979. In 1983 it was published again, this time under the author's title, which we use here, as part of* Fears, *edited by Charles L. Grant, and issued by Berkley Books, New York.*

Some of us on The Team don't even know that it exists. We're never told about it when we're hired; nor are we ever given the *real* reasons for our hiring. And those of us (like me) who do catch on, seldom even discuss it with each other. On paper, The Team doesn't exist at all. It permeates other agencies; we shuffle filing cards, or act as couriers, or translate documents, or diddle with computers, and each of us has been checked very, *very* carefully where security is concerned, not only by the hush-hush people but by Colonel Samuel Warhorse, who either is or isn't a displaced Army medic, and who once or twice a year goes back to Oklahoma to do his thing as a Medicine Chief of the Osage Nation, and who'd be captain of The Team *if* it existed, just as I'd be his second-in-command.

The best way to describe it is by using the example of water departments and their dowsers. Just about every major city water department has one or more dowsers on its payroll — but never *as* dowsers, because water-witching still isn't quite respectable. They're hired as backhoe operators, or truck drivers, or whatever, and there they are, ready to do their real job when necessary.

That's how it is with us. Somehow our real jobs filter in to us, always through Chief Sam, and we tackle them and do our best, and afterwards everybody forgets all about them, just as people forget about water department dowsers when they fill their bathtubs.

What sort of jobs? Problems that defy ordinary, logical solutions. Puzzles that make no sense. Perils materializing for no reason out of nowhere. Disasters that simply cannot be, but *are*.

For instance—

Chief Sam called me at 11:30. "We've got another one, Garry," he said. "Smells like a real collector's item. How's about lunch at noon?"

I didn't argue I already had a date. I cancelled it, and half an hour later, when he walked into the chop house with two other characters, I was waiting for him.

I stood up, and he introduced them. Two were state police captains, one out from Pennsylvania, the other a tall, rangy, local Western type named Tod Welles; the third, with a French name and nice manners, was an R.C.M.P. [Royal Canadian Mounted Police] superintendent from up across the border.

"Douglas Garrioch," Sam told them. "He used to be a fly-boy. Sometimes he turns out to be pretty useful." He grinned at me, his eyes black-agate under his black sequoia eyebrows and gray hair, and slapped me on the shoulder with a hand like a bear-paw. We ordered

The Beasts that Perish

drinks, making small-talk till the waiter brought them. Then there was silence. I looked at him.

"Our problem for the day," he said, "is simply stated. "During the past week, the fatal one-car accident rate has suddenly gone up — by four-thousand eight-hundred and some-odd percent."

"Where?" I asked.

"The entire United States and all of Canada. Garry, that means that almost fifty times as many people as usual have started smashing their cars into concrete abutments, plunging them into rivers, rolling them down cliffs — and at top speeds. And at night, *only* at night. Folks are getting spooked. Insurance companies are already having fits. The press is starting to get too damn interested and making noises. So far, nobody's released the real statistics, but there's no way to keep the local police and sheriffs quiet. It's lucky winter's almost on us, so there's weather to blame it on, but the story's sure to break wide open before too long — and we just can't afford that kind of panic."

"So?" I said, feeling those familiar small cold feet along my back.

"So you go back to work. You dig right in and find what's going on, and just who's killing whom — if there *is* a who. The boys here'll fill you in on everything they know. It's yours from there. Now let's have lunch."

They told me while we ate. They were experts in their field, specialists on highway accidents, and they had all the facts and figures at their fingertips, all the hows and wheres and whens— and nothing else, no *whys*. I asked the obvious questions, trying to find a pattern that'd link everything together.

The Timeless Tales of Reginald Bretnor

What about the drivers? What kind of people were they? That angle had been pretty thoroughly explored; they were just about every kind. The only thing they seemed to have in common was that most of them had done a lot of freeway driving — the percentage of big-rig truckers was astonishing — but there were too many exceptions to lay down a rule. Otherwise, they were of all ages, sexes, races, driving every kind of car or truck and a few motorcycles. Almost always, they had been alone, or just about alone, on the road, with the next vehicle at least half a mile away; and always, *always* they had been going way over the limit— estimated speed 80, 85, 90, sometimes about a hundred.

How about passengers? Well, there'd been just a few, no bus loads, no big groups, not even any foursomes— and all strictly in the past tense when found.

"Any last words?" I asked. "Did any of 'em drop any kind of hint about what happened? About what might've hit 'em?" And I was told that no, they hadn't, not really. There'd been a salesman in Ohio somewhere who was still alive when they pulled him out; they thought he screamed out something about hitting a coyote before he coughed up blood and died, but they weren't sure, and anyhow no coyotes had been anywhere around those parts since frontier days.

Besides him, there was just a doctor in Saskatchewan, out on the motel circuit with his office nurse; she had lived long enough to whisper something that sounded like "squirrel... squirrel... squirrel..."

"The birds and the beasts were there," quoted Chief Sam. "An odd coincidence."

The Beasts that Perish

"Odd— but hardly pertinent," the R.C.M.P. man shrugged. "People say weird things when they're dying."

And that was that. They had no more to add. Chief Sam and I walked them to the door after he'd paid the check, and he said how I'd keep in touch with them, with Welles especially, and how they'd pass on all reports to me; and I guess somebody had briefed them— they asked no questions about how we'd operate. Then the Chief and I went back into the bar for one more drink and my instructions.

"Hit the road, Garry," he said. "Tonight and every night, till you find out something. Stay on the freeways, particularly the Interstates. There've been a few bad ones on back-country roads, but its the freeways where everything's been really happening. Here are your credentials, state *and* federal." He grinned. "They're sort of hoked up for the occasion, but they're genuine and guaranteed to impress everybody, even us Honest Injuns." He handed me two cards and an enamel-and-gold badge. "They make out you're sort of a cross between Ralph Nader, Oh-Oh-Seven, and the ghost of J. Edgar Hoover. Don't throw their weight around unless you have to."

"Thank you, Heroic Leader," I said, knocking off my drink. "You've put me in the ticket-fixing business. Now I can make my fortune and retire, and take Marina on a trip around the world."

"Any time," said Chief Sam, "*after* you stop those folks getting themselves killed off. Now don't forget to fill your tank— you're going to need it." His grin disappeared. "Take care, Garry, and give that lovely girl of yours my love."

The Timeless Tales of Reginald Bretnor

I drove back to the office, and checked out early; and drove slowly up to the apartment, thinking about The Team, and Chief Sam and Marina and myself, and how the strangeness of our natures and our backgrounds and our lives had brought us together to do jobs that needed doing and otherwise would never have been done.

Take me, for instance— three of my grandparents were of Scotch descent, by way of Nova Scotia; the fourth was French and English mixed. And there was second-sight on both sides of the family. My great-grandfather Garrioch had seen visions, and known when death would come for friends and relatives there in the cold Western Isles.

His son, my grandfather, had it also; but it was different in him, for almost never was it conscious. Usually it simply guided him in simple acts, things done or not done to keep one out of danger; he fought four years as an infantryman in World War I, in the Black Watch, and lived to emigrate— very nearly a survival record.

My father inherited it again, and it protected him after he moved down to New England to fish the harsh Atlantic, and in the Navy all through the Second War.

In my case it again had changed. I didn't know I had it until I took my first tour as a chopper pilot in Vietnam. Yes, it protected me— but it also told me, quite consciously and definitely, when death was going to strike— when Charlie was going to slam his rockets or mortar shells into the base, and who on any mission wouldn't make it back.

What do you do with that kind of talent? You don't report yourself to Headquarters. No, you worry about it, and maybe drop a hint to a close friend or two when

The Beasts that Perish

you feel they'd ought to hit the sick list, and grieve when they won't take your advice and end up dead. Then, if like me you're very, *very* lucky, maybe you run into someone like Chief Sam. He was doing his stuff there at the great base hospital in Saigon, and I was taking a routine physical; and next thing I knew somehow I'd told him everything, and his advice had been simply to accept it, to say nothing, and to keep in touch. We'd be seeing more of one another, he said.

So there I was, driving home to my golden girl, thinking that if it hadn't been for him probably I never would've met her. She had been born in Hawaii, on Maui, her father an Icelander, her mother Japanese, and she was golden-skinned and glowing, and so delicate that she looked almost breakable. She was as sensitive as a Gothic heroine, and as tough as whalebone.

She had to be. *Her* talent had just missed being her tragedy. She is an empath. Even as a child, she could feel— in each degree, in every terrible detail— the agony of others. Not physical pain itself, but its tormenting tensions and its terrors, the futile thrashings of trapped minds trying to cope with other kinds of pain.

It is a talent unhappily too common, and children born with it often become autistic, withdrawing totally into themselves, for in societies that deny and fear the extrasensory, they have no way of learning how to distinguish between exterior agonies and those genuinely their own.

But Marina's parents were wise enough to listen, wise enough not to put her down. They had no rules to follow, so— instead of calling in the headshrinkers— when she was seven they took her to her grandmother in Japan, who had retired to a convent for Zen Buddhist nuns. There she was cared for until she was 14, visited at least twice a year by one or another of her parents and in constant touch with all her Japanese relations. And there she learned, not how or why her talent came to be, but how she herself, her being, her spirit, could live with it and maintain tranquility.

When she returned to her father and mother in Hawaii, it had in no way been suppressed, but now she knew how to avoid the dangerous chains of emotional identification, how to say, "This agony's not mine, *it is not me*," how not to react to it.

And yet a visit to a hospital was still, for her, an act of heroism, and she would ask me to detour for miles rather than pass a penitentiary, an insane asylum, a slaughterhouse. For her talent differs from ordinary telepathy; distance is an important factor in it, and so are numbers. She can handle the impact of suffering individuals well enough, but groups still can overwhelm her. She cannot heal; except very rarely, with people whom she loves, she is powerless even to ameliorate. She can only feel.

In the islands, she went through high school and then on to college, taking a degree in librarianship— a wise choice, for libraries have more books than people, and books, whatever torments they contain, don't broadcast them. Then she got a job stateside, at a small college library in eastern Washington; and that was where Chief Sam ran into her— by accident, of course, the way he always seems to find his people. He was asking her a question at the reference desk when, without warning, she just came out of gear, leaving the conversation dangling. She turned deathly pale; her pupils dilated; she

The Beasts that Perish

gasped for breath. It took her several minutes to pull herself together, while he watched.

And then they heard the sirens. Some self-tortured kid, stoked up on speed and LSD and God knows what, had climbed the campanile tower and tried to fly. She had tuned in him in that first dreadful second when he had found that he could not.

Chief Sam coaxed it all out of her, and found her a new library job at a nice quiet computer center in Cinnabar, the little Colorado mining town half grown up where The Team works— still small enough so that you aren't psychically snowed under as you are in, say, Chicago or New York, but big enough to hold those government subagencies we need to keep us going plausibly.

He introduced us. I saw her glowing skin, her strange, green-golden eyes, her hair like the fine black lacquer of a household shrine in ancient Nara, and instantly I knew the joy and fire of her temperament, and the tempered strength under her gentleness and her fragility. We drew together, feeling one another before we had so much as touched our hands; and it was wonderful that neither she nor I, nor Chief Sam even — neither then nor later — had to conceal why we were there, what we were all about.

That made it a whole lot easier, for we needed no barriers of security between us. I could tell her exactly what I was getting myself into, just as she could tell me. So as soon as I got home I phoned her on the job and asked her to take the rest of the afternoon off. I filled her in on the whole deal, and told her there'd probably be nights I'd have to spend away from home. She shook her shining head, and smiled ruefully. "I guess there's just no limit to the things some men won't do to get out of making love to their poor, lonely wives," she said.

And of course, with that, I had to pick her up, laughing in my arms, and carry her into the bedroom.

We went to dinner early, and I told her everything again, somehow hoping that she might, intuitively, think of an angle we had missed. Those drivers, I repeated, driving at top speeds and late at night, must've seen *something*, something startling enough to make them swerve suicidally. The only alternative was to believe spooks were riding with them, or flying saucer people were suddenly controlling them, or the Russkies or Red Chinese were playing with a new secret weapon. For a few moments, she responded with that look people get when they are searching in themselves, but when she spoke it was only to say that she didn't like the freeways.

"I'm not happy on them," she said, looking a little puzzled. "There's— well, there's something *wrong* about them. But it's too vague. I can't get hold of it. It's only strong enough to make me feel uneasy." She took my hand in both of hers. "I know it's silly of me, Garry, with your— your talent. But you *will* be careful, won't you? Promise me?"

It was six days to Thanksgiving. The weather had been nasty for a week, but the night was clear. The highways had dried off, and though yesterday's snow blanketed trees, houses, hillsides, when I reached I-25 it was all clear going and the traffic was moving ten miles an hour faster than the law allowed, with the big rigs and some other drivers pushing even beyond that.

I got my first signal around 10 o'clock, near a side road leading to a little town called Penfield, so I followed

The Beasts that Perish

my nose down the off-ramp, and within three miles I came to it— a crazy, telescoped VW van, crushed against a cruelly jagged rock-face. There was a wrecker there, and two state police cars, and a sheriff's deputy, so I pulled off and showed the sergeant my credentials. He was properly impressed and treated me like I wish people had when I was in the Army.

"Another one of these goddam one-car deals," he commented, "and not even on the freeway. Lucky it's just a lousy hippie down the drain— probably higher than a kite on something. He's on his way to Penfield in the meat-wagon."

I spent 15 minutes with him, and though he kept repeating we wouldn't find a thing, he did help me search the area; and he was right, of course. There wasn't anything.

"I wish to God we could've found it," he said. "Just once, to take the curse off this crazy business. If you're working on it, I sure wish you luck. Believe me, it's getting to us all!"

That was the first of five that night. The second was just about a duplicate, right off an interchange on 25, only the car looked like it'd been brand new and probably a Cadillac. The third was a huge diesel truck lying on its crushed cab at the foot of a steep embankment; I got there almost right away, even before the ambulance, and it was a messy deal— messy enough to shake me and the two policemen. The next was standard— a concrete overpass, ripped chunks of what had been a passionate Porche, a young man's body underneath a blanket. The fifth was something else again— a flaming, smoking heap of unidentifiable wreckage half a straight mile down the mountain side, with the cops and me and the trucker who'd reported it staring helplessly and talking about getting a crew down there come morning.

There were no clues at any of them.

I'd called Marina before midnight from a coffee stop, to tell her where I was and that I loved her; and by 3 a.m., more than a hundred miles from home, I holed up in a flea-bag motel, ate a sandwich, drank half a pint of bourbon, and hit the sack.

I slept till noon — after all, my working hours were going to be from dark to dawn — then made my calls to Chief Sam and Tod Welles, and learned that there was nothing new except a scare story in a national tabloid, which wasn't making anybody happy. I spent the afternoon talking the situation over with state and local police, doing none of us much good, and had dinner with a superannuated sheriff who'd actually forbidden his wife and kids to use the highways after dark.

That night was like the first, only there were seven of them instead of five; it had rained and snowed a little, and we had bad slick spots here and there. I drove where instinct told me, and again learned nothing.

For the next three days, the pattern scarcely varied. I followed 25 clear up into Wyoming and back down again. I followed I-70 for almost 300 miles west of Denver, coping with more bad weather, bedding down at night with my bit of bourbon to dream about Marina — with a nightmare or two about fatal crashes to keep me on my toes. I had nothing to report except somebody's testimony at third hand from the state police, who'd had it from a sheriff's deputy, who had it from a shepherd type driving an old pickup: he'd been following one of them maybe a quarter-mile away, and he thought maybe he'd seen some sort of shadow moving right in front of her before she hit.

Then, late on the fourth night, after 2 a.m., I pulled into a truck stop to get myself together. I'd just come from the nastiest wreck of all — a truck and trailer filled with something flammable. It had gone off at a sharp curve, hit some trees and flamed instantly. I was there long before the police arrived — in time to hear the driver screaming — and there was absolutely nothing I could do but watch the flames. When it was over, I went into the truck-stop restaurant, ordered a T-bone and coffee to drink while it was cooking, drank half the coffee, filled the cup up again from a pint I kept against emergencies, and found myself listening to four truckers in the booth behind me. They were fresh off the road, and they knew the man whom I'd heard die.

They made the usual profane comments about the one-car crack-ups, only they said one-rig instead, and they indulged in the same foolish and futile attempts to explain them, or explain them away. Then, "Goddamit, okay!" growled one of them. "That was a hell of a way to go, but — ah crap, man! If it had to happen could you have picked any guy you'd rather have it happen to?"

"Don't talk like that, Slavich," barked another. "Grayber was a bastard, sure he was, but Jesus! — he was human, wasn't he?"

"Human? Like sour owl shit he was human! Remember how that poor damn girl of his always looked like she'd been beat up on? Well, she had. And talk to anybody who's rode with him, or right behind him even. Twice I seen him try to nudge cars off the road when he figured nobody was looking. And he'd run over every critter crossed the road ahead of him — dog, cat, possum, you name it. The sonnabitch'd speed up to catch 'em. He'd swerve to cut 'em down. Hell, for my money he had it coming!"

They kept on arguing about the dead Grayber for a bit, with nobody getting really mad about it, and then the talk changed to women, and I quit listening. I ate my steak — a good one — but somehow it didn't really grab me. I kept remembering that driver in Ohio who'd screamed about hitting a coyote, and the nurse in Canada who'd died mumbling "squirrel... squirrel... squirrel..." My mind just wouldn't chase the thought away. When I drove off, I told myself to stop imagining a connection. Sure, there'd been people who'd killed themselves trying to keep from running down a dog, but chances were most had been inexperienced drivers.

There was only one more that night; and next day, when I phoned in, Chief Sam told me to come on back for Thanksgiving. Marina and I could have the night together, and then next day, unless we had a date, would we have dinner with his family?

I told him we were free as air, we'd love to; and then he told me that he and Tod Welles had been taking Emmie Bostwick to every crash site they could think of. She was part of The Team, a black girl from around Baton Rouge, with a genius for sensing felonious little plans being hatched or carried out anywhere near her — even a day or two afterwards.

She had a courier's job, a good cover for sudden travelling, and the Chief used her when terrorists or blackmailers were making threats. She was pretty close to being infallible; and she'd detected nothing, absolutely nothing. Chief Sam felt that if there was dirty work afoot

The Beasts that Perish

it was a long-range deal, and it might even help for me to take a two-day break.

So I called Marina and gave her the good news, and in her voice I could read not only pleasure but relief. "Oh, I'm glad, lover! At least I'll have you off those freeways for awhile. Last night I had an awful dream — I guess it wasn't really *awful*, but in the dream it was. It scared me, and I've been worried for you ever since. Garry, don't laugh — I dreamed you ran over a poor raccoon."

I didn't laugh, partly because once I had; and, coming home, I drove more carefully than I usually do.

Thanksgiving Day, I took time out in the afternoon to get together with Tod Welles and his R.C.M.P. friend and compare notes. We told each other what we could, and ended up just where we'd started, on line one. Then, at around 4:30, Marina and I drove out to the Warhorses'. Chief Sam has about 20 acres a dozen miles out of Cinnabar, near a weird little place called Dudgeon, where there's nothing but a service station, a general store, a bar, a hashhouse, and a combination city hall and volunteer fire department— but only half a mile off the good main road, where you can snake around the mountains without losing too much speed and with about half of it freeway so nobody can really hold you up. It didn't take us long to get there; there wasn't even a whisper of bad weather.

We were greeted by Chief Sam, his wife Connie, three kids, a pretty Warhorse cousin from some university out West, two big brown Labs, a Siamese, and a striped tabby cat. The Warhorses told us it was heap good for stupid palefaces to come in out of the cold and drink firewater with the friendly natives; and we all sat there before the huge fireplace, surrounded by dogs and cats and kids, talking, laughing, and forgetting that along the miles of road that hold our world together people were suddenly smashing to their deaths.

Our conversation flowed from one culture into another; tales were told born in traditions continents apart. Nobody spoiled things by trying to hog the floor; when disagreements showed themselves they became friendly fencing matches instead of duels. Then we went in to dinner, and let the turkey dictate to us.

We left just after midnight, still glowing, and at the door we were kissed goodnight; and when I shook Chief Sam's hand I knew that he, even as I myself, at once regretted that tomorrow it would be back to work— and looked forward to it.

The night was frosty; the air was crystal clear; never had there been so many stars across the sky. Quickly, we left Dudgeon sound asleep behind us, and in moments we were at the freeway entrance. I turned into it. I speeded up. And, as I did so, I felt again, suddenly, that something was all set to happen— and the feeling, as it always is, was laced with fear.

"*Damn!*" I said, only half aloud. "Not *tonight!*"

Marina heard me. "Garry," she whispered, "are you sure?"

The feeling, oddly, was a little different. I couldn't tell exactly how, but that didn't change it. "Yes, I'm sure," I told her. "I wish to God I wasn't, but I am."

"Can't you— can't we ignore it?"

I shook my head. In the rearview mirror I could see the single light of a motorcycle coming, coming fast.

The Beasts that Perish

That's him! I thought, as he swept by, doing 80 or 85— and yet, somehow, I wasn't sure it *was* him. Still, whatever it might be, I knew that he was part of it.

"This one may be special," I told her, stepping on the gas. "There's something strange about it. We'll have to see."

She didn't say a word. Her hand moved over and rested lightly on my knee.

For three miles we followed him, taking the mad curves, never letting him get more than half a mile away. Then we came to a long, straight, downhill stretch. We passed a sign saying JEFFERS PASS, TURNOFF 2 MI. There ahead of us was the interchange, a concrete bastion pierced by two sally-ports. Our motorcyclist was heading straight toward it. I could feel apprehension building in me. I could feel the tightening of Marina's hand against my thigh.

The concrete rushed toward the motorcyclist. It rushed at us. It seemed to grow. There was the second sign. There, very suddenly, was the turnoff.

And, so abruptly that for an instant I thought he'd lose control, the motorcyclist hit his brakes and, tires shrieking, swerved sharply to the right, taking the turnoff, barely making it. I forced my eyes back to the road in front of me. I heard Marina scream—

In my headlights, right in the middle of my lane, less than a hundred feet ahead of me, there was a wildcat, white fangs bared, ears back, eyes burning bright—

And he was 25 feet high.

How many impressions can you crowd into a quarter-second? How many decisions can you make in half that time? I recall Marina screaming; my hands doing their damndest to twist the wheel; my brain, in shock, still forcing them to freeze, forcing my foot to floor the throttle instead of trying for the brake. I remember my mind telling me that cats are not as hard as concrete. I don't recall whether or not I closed my eyes. We hit. There was no impact, none. There was a timeless instant in which I felt surrounded by flesh and fur, by the idea of fur and flesh, by an animal odor, musky and far away. Then we were through, and through beneath the overpass, and nothing lay ahead of us but open road. I looked up in the mirror, and there was nothing there.

Then the reaction hit me. Fearing that in a moment I would be trembling uncontrollably, I let my foot leave the throttle. I let compression slow us down. Finally I pulled off onto the shoulder, stopped the car with a jerk.

Beside me, Marina's scream had dropped to a small, wailing moan, ululating hysterically. I switched the engine off. Trying to control my almost spastic hands and arms, I reached for her.

"Darling, *darling!*" I cried out, shaking her by the shoulders. "It's all right! We're safe! Everything's all right!"

She stared at me out of enormous eyes. Her moaning stopped. "Let me *go!*" she cried out, pulling violently away. Then she covered up her face and wept, her head thrown back, her whole body shaken with her weeping.

"Sweetheart! Marina! It's all *right!*" I kept repeating foolishly. "It was a hologram— some kind of a projection. That's *all* it was. I tell you, we're *safe.* There's no need to be afraid!"

She dropped her hands. Still weeping, she threw herself at me. "Afraid? *Afraid?* Of course I'm not afraid! What was there there for me to be afraid of?" Her small fists hammered at my shoulder, at my chest. "My G-G-

The Beasts that Perish

God, are you a log? A stone? *C-can't you feel anything at all?*"

I simply stared at her, helpless before her terrifying intensity.

"My God, *my G-G-God!*" she sobbed, covering her face again. "Those animals! Those poor, *poor* animals! Oh, God, when I think of the c-callousness, the utter emptiness, the— the abandonment, the *uselessness!* Oh, damn you, *damn you!* You'll never understand!"

Once more, her weeping shook her; and I, shaken by her words, made no attempt to touch her. An endless minute passed, lacerated by her sobbing, a minute and another and a third— then suddenly it was over. She dropped her hands again; she sighed, a sound so sad and so forlorn that any hurt I might have felt was swept away. Gently, she reached out to me.

"I never should have said that," she whispered. "Garry, not to *you*. I'm sorry. It's just— just that you're a Westerner. In Asia, we see things differently. Besides, though you can see perils in the future, *I*— I share agonies right *now*. Have you ever thought what we've been doing to the animals? On every highway, Garry? We run them down, but it's not death that counts—" Her hands clutched at mine. "We all die, men and beasts. In the wilds, an animal will die, and it'll be eaten, by other beasts, and birds of prey, and scavenging insects. At least its substance goes to sustain more life."

"How about men killed in war?" I said. "By earthquakes, tidal waves, tornadoes?"

"We're on a different level. Most of us. Animals *have* to feel their deaths aren't purposeless." Her voice rose. "Garry, did you know that sometimes one *caribou* will actually allow a pack of wolves to eat it? That antelopes in Africa have done the same for hunting lions? They *know*. They know it in the group-souls they share, life after life, until they individualize as men. I know you don't believe that, but it's what Buddhists teach—"

She stroked my face; she let me hold her close. "What have we done to them, for years and years, as our highway speeds went up and our concern went down? Have you ever seen a dead animal even thrown off a freeway, Garry— except deer, because they're big enough to cause accidents? No, no! We leave them there, to be crushed, flattened thin, rubbed into the fabric of our concrete— even their hair, their hides— until they vanish. No other animals can get to them to profit by their deaths, not even buzzards— no, not even ants! And that is what they do not understand, their useless dying, the contemptuous coldness of our disregard; and in their chilly emptiness they hate us for it. More and more and more of them. They— they've reached critical mass. It was no hologram that tried to kill us! They're striking back!"

I thought about Jung's theory of group-souls. I remembered the stories of Lord Buddha, feeding his own body to hungry tigers.

"Garry, you've seen Kuniyoshi's prints of monster cats! You've heard the legends, from every continent, of monster dogs and jaguars and wolves! They aren't just legends. They're *real*— but never, never, *never* on this scale. Lover, you *must* believe me. *You must, you must!* I felt it all when— when we went through that beast."

I did remember the legends I had read. Even the one about the monstrous cat that's said to haunt the lower corridors of the Capitol in Washington— still terrifying patrolling guards at night. I remembered, and in spite of

The Beasts that Perish

logic, in spite of my own training— and also just because I knew my girl so well— I did believe.

"Marina," I said then, "what can we do?"

"In Japan," she told me, "the people who grow cultured pearls have *segaki* services performed for the spirits of all those oysters who die in making them. Samisen makers have them said for the dogs and cats whose skins are stretched over their instruments. It is an explanation, an apology. That is all they ask."

"Who could we get to do it here? Christianity tells us animals have no souls. You know, '*the beasts that perish.*'"

"Not all Christians believe that," she answered, "nor all ministers, and there are many others who would help."

"And how are we supposed to sell Chief Sam on the idea?"

She kissed me, there next to the haunted highway. "We'll have no trouble there," she declared. "*His* people never did deny that animals have souls."

It took Chief Sam a little while to get things organized, especially without stirring up a mess of controversy. But he managed it, and we were surprised at how many people from how many different faiths came to our assistance. (The media hardly touched it, and when they did they treated it as nut stuff, as a joke.) Within ten days, the one-car fatal accident rate had plummeted; in three weeks it had returned to normal. In a month, almost everyone had forgotten it completely, and I was trying to.

Then, in February, the Chief and I had to take Emmie Bostwick up to Denver to check out an anonymous assassination warning, which turned out to be baseless. We had an early supper and headed back, praying that the roads would all be dry and open. We did have bad weather for the first two hours; then it cleared and before we knew it the traffic was all passing us, trying to make up time.

Our first hint of trouble came around 10 o'clock, when the feeling came to me. I thought, "Jesus, not *again!*" — still seeing that wildcat in my mind's eye. Then, to my relief, Emmie started breathing hoarsely, as she always does when one of her impressions starts coming through. "I get a great big car like, or maybe it's a bus," she told us. "It's full of men, just men. They— oh, they scare me! Something's gonna happen! One of 'em's up front, where he oughtn't be, up past the— I guess it's wire— and— *oh, no, no! Don't you do it!* Oh, Chief Sam, he's goin' to do something to the driver— with a knife! And—" She shuddered and was silent. "Man! I'm sure glad *that's* gone," she muttered finally.

Chief Sam soothed her, and we drove on. It was a full hour before we saw the traffic block, the blue lights, ambulances, wreckers, all clustered around an overpass. I swung our own light down against the windshield, and on the shoulder we passed the long halted line. We stopped behind a knot of police cars. Sam and I got out. The freeway for a hundred yards was strewn with shattered metal, torn metal, twisted metal, metal charred out of all recognition, shattered glass, and— well, other things. Above it all, there was a great gap in the railing of the overpass.

We found Tod Welles there, in charge. He filled us in. "At least, Colonel," he told Sam, "it's not a one-car

The Beasts that Perish

deal, so you don't have to worry, but it's really going to be a bugger to clean up. The bus—"

The bus had been state owned, on its way from Andriess Hospital, maximum security for the criminally insane, loaded with more than thirty of their hopeless cases— all kinky killers who had killed again inside, or tried to. They were being moved to a special new even-more-maximum facility, and one of them— though nobody could figure how— had gotten to the driver and cut his throat—

Sam and I looked at one another, thinking of Emmie.

—and the bus had plunged straight down into the path of a truck and trailer loaded with steel pipe, trying to make 90 miles an hour. It was like being hit by an express train—

Welles gestured at the road. "Two survivors," he told us. "One guard, one prisoner. About a dozen of the bodies are sort of in one piece. The rest have all been through the shredder. And now it's fixing up to snow." He gestured at a few flakes that had started falling. "We'll be lucky to get the big hunks found and the road opened before a storm hits."

The wrecker crews were hauling and pushing metal off the highway; the ambulance men, some carrying stretchers, some with baskets, were going about their grimmer business.

Welles kept looking at his watch. "At least," he said, "it's not like we were dealing with real people, except the driver and the guards. Those bastards were subhuman, every damn one of 'em. No loss." He shrugged. "Hell, what we can't find of them the big rigs'll take care of."

The Timeless Tales of Reginald Bretnor

Chief Sam and I looked at each other once again, and I knew that he and I were thinking the same thing, and I could feel gooseflesh all along my arms.

Then he took Tod Welles aside, and spoke to him quietly and very seriously; and we left him there after we'd said goodnight.

"What's he going to do?" I asked, as we walked back.

"He's going to stay till every piece is found— each ear, each finger-bone, each scrap of flesh. He doesn't understand, but he'll do what I asked him to." He drew a deep breath. "Garry," he said, "there are some things we mustn't take a chance on. Not *ever*."

9
Without (General) Issue

"Without (General) Issue" was published in Isaac Asimov's Science Fiction Magazine 5, *Nov. 23, 1981. This is the story's first appearance in a book.*

Gentlemen, you have summoned me to explain to your committee why I, as commander-in-chief, absolutely will not permit women officers as members of Space Force First Contact teams.

Very well, I shall tell you.

It goes back to when I was a new lieutenant, fresh out of the Academy, assigned to my first team. There were five of us: Captain Arkleigh, the C.O.; Jameson and Clavijo, both techs; myself; and Hildreth, our telepath. Then, of course, there was Hildreth's symbiote, a gray cat named Richelieu. As I'm sure you know, in those days we were forced to depend even more on telepaths than we are today, and they always relied partly on their animals. Cats and dogs are telepathically sensitive on primitive levels normally closed to humans, and they in turn can communicate what they sense to us, or at least to telepaths adequately trained.

Our probes had reported a fantastic mishmash of electronic emissions from the seventh planet of a star called Alpha-Poronis— if you want, I can pinpoint it for you on the star charts.

The Timeless Tales of Reginald Bretnor

That will not be necessary? Thank you, gentlemen.

Naturally, everybody at Headquarters was very excited because it was accepted that structured electronic activity on what had to be communications frequencies meant technological progress of a very high order, and our team was ordered to go and introduce ourselves to the civilization producing it.

We orbited the planet, which was astoundingly Earth-like— a 17.682 similarity factor, to put it in present-day terms— and sent in a lander. We had seen nothing to indicate that our new friends had achieved either space flight or space weaponry, but we kept electronic silence on their known frequencies as a precaution.

At any rate, nobody bothered the lander, and for some days it kept sending us its pictures, reports, and analyses. It had come down on what I can only describe as a meadow, even if the grass wasn't really grass as we know it, and the surrounding trees weren't really trees. You know how extraterrestrial vegetation usually differs from ours, just strange enough to be subtly disturbing. But there was nothing — absolutely nothing — dangerous to man. The air was breathable; the bacteria were too alien to affect us; there were no signs of predators or anything poisonous; several of the vegetable growths analyzed by the lander actually turned out to be "probably edible." The only living creatures observed were spheroid. They looked like grayish-green puffballs, and they moved by just rolling around, pushing themselves with small anatomical jets — just farting along, if you'll forgive my use of the term.

But that wasn't all they could do. They were able to extrude usable tentacles, stand up on them, manipulated objects and, so it appeared, each other. They were

Without (General) Issue

also able to extrude what I can only call eye-things, in clusters of two to a dozen. They differed in size from eight or ten inches to about three to four feet, and they were busy as bird dogs, rolling, and getting up to their tentacles, and dancing around to touch each other. Not only that, but some distance away the lander's cameras showed us definite structures, with what seemed to be woven roofs and transparent mesh walls.

There was no doubt about it. They were intelligent, and they seemed to be more or less civilized. Arkleigh gave the order, and we went down, hovering just long enough to get the lay of the land. At one end of the meadow, there was a wide stream, and it was so pretty that he decided to set down beside it. Had it not been for the much-too-green sky, the place would have looked just like home.

From then on, we went by the book. The puffballs looked up as we landed, eyed us for a moment or two, and went back to what they'd been doing. Obviously, they didn't take our vessel for a Chariot of the Gods out of space.

"All right," Arkleigh said. "Hildreth, let Richelieu out."

We were all anxious to see what would happen, and we had our noses glued to the ports as Hildreth opened the hatch and let down the catwalk.

Richelieu took a good, hearty sniff of the nice, clean alien air, hoisted his tail, let out an exuberant *meow!* and walked out majestically. Twenty feet from the catwalk he paused, surveying the scene.

Now, abruptly, everything changed. The puffballs stopped simultaneously. All together, they extruded their eye-things. They stood up on their tentacles. All together, they danced forward, forming a semicircle around us. They were all looking at Richelieu.

"Getting anything, Hildreth?" Arkleigh asked.

"Sir," Hildreth whispered excitedly. "They— they're *admiring* him. Watch him! He knows it. Cats love admiration—"

Delicately, Richelieu lifted a paw, stuck out his pink tongue, and started to wash.

"No doubt about it?"

"None, sir. None at all. I can almost feel it myself."

"Then out you go!" Arkleigh told him.

Richelieu broke off washing. He had seen that the banks of the stream were sandy, and he hadn't had a chance to dig into fresh sand since our takeoff. He stalked over to it, sniffed, dug his hole, squatted over it, did his business, filled the hole in enthusiastically, and took a long drink of the water.

In the meantime, Hildreth had followed him out.

"Can *you* contact them?" Arkleigh called to him.

"Sir, I've been trying to, but they pay no attention. I'm pretty sure they aren't telepathic. But I'm getting impressions from *them*. Not very clear ones. It's about like trying to read the mind of a porpoise. But they're aware of me, and— well, they admire me too. They think I'm wonderful!"

"Better be careful, Joe" Clavijo called out. "They'll be forming a fan club."

"Shut up!" Arkleigh told him. "Hindreth, do you get any danger signals— anger, fear, hunger, hostility?"

"None at all, sir."

Well, gentlemen, again we went by the book. We all filed out. After all, we had side-arms.

Without (General) Issue

We lined up next to Hildreth, and Arkleigh stepped forward.

"Take me to your leader!" whispered Clavijo, and the Captain told him again to shut up.

The puffballs were coming closer and closer, holding each other's tentacles like a ring of schoolgirls holding hands— closer and closer—

"Still no hostility?" Arkleigh asked anxiously.

"Absolutely not!" Hildreth told him.

And that's when it happened.

Gentlemen, this has been classified "TOP SECRET" ever since, and I trust that no word of it will get beyond this committee. All I felt was an infinitesimal instant of unendurable tension— and the next thing I knew I was lying on my back— on my *bare* back, gentlemen — and my head felt like a bursting balloon. Slowly, I made myself look around. We were all on our backs, Captain Arkleigh, and Jameson and Clavijo, and I, and Hildreth. And we were all naked — all except Richelieu, who at least still had his fur coat on.

Jameson looked at me with one bloodshot eye. "Bill," he gasped, "wh— what *happened*? Where *are* we?"

I looked around. We were lying in the middle of what was only too clearly a cage of some sort of translucent fibers, roofed with a similar stuff closely woven. The cage was about 20' by 30', or perhaps a bit more, and one corner of it was occupied by an eight-foot-square sandbox. It was surrounded by a whole crowd of puffballs, all standing up on their tentacles and pushing in for a really good look.

"*Where are we?*" Jameson repeated hysterically.

"I think," I told him, "we've landed in what the locals use for a zoo."

The Timeless Tales of Reginald Bretnor

Gentlemen, we were there *for more than two years*. In the back wall of the cage, they'd put a crawl-through door that led into a sort of cave, but it was kept closed during business hours, so our only privacy was at night. Of course, at first we did our best to communicate with our captors, but it was utterly useless. They used no verbal symbols. They used no visual symbols. We concluded that they were living computers, living electronic devices. They chattered by touching tentacles or by using whatever passed for their CB bands. But when we tried to get through to them by scratching a Pythagorean theorem on the floor of the cage, or demonstrating our knowledge of universal mathematical truths, all they did was hold up the tinier puffballs so they could see better.

Of course, we tried to escape — but we soon learned our lesson. When we put any strain on those fibers — any at all — we got another jolt of whatever had knocked us out the first time.

They fed us — not too badly if you like strange raw vegetables and occasionally raw fish from the river — there seemed to be fish everywhere — and they gave us plenty of fresh water and cleaned the sandbox out every night. And, gentlemen, how would *you* like to use a goddam catbox for your sanitary purposes, especially with a few hundred puffballs watching you with their unwinking eyes? Because Richelieu had been first out, they must have taken him for our leader and assumed we'd all do as he did.

It may seem funny to you here and now, but it sure as hell wasn't funny to us. We could see our spaceship, untouched in the distance, and Hildreth didn't make things any better by assuring us that the puffballs sim-

Without (General) Issue

ply *adored* us— I guess like kids adore the monkey-islands in our own zoos.

I will say Hildreth never gave up. He kept right on trying to get through to them, and doing his best to catch what they were thinking, but all he could ever latch onto were bits of what he called parallel emotions, like a sort of fondness for each other and their littler puffballs, and that stupid business about how they loved us.

How did we pass the time? Gentlemen, we told stories. We made up games, as well as we could without so much as a scrap of paper or a stick or a stone. We gave each other IQ tests. We shared our knowledge of this and that, or did our best to.

And we were *bored* — bored almost to extinction. We tried hard to keep up our spirits and each other's. Catbox and all, with hair to our shoulders and beards to our middles, we still tried to maintain man's dignity. But more and more often we found dark despair overwhelming us. The only reason none of us tried to commit suicide was because there was nothing to do it with.

Then one morning we came out of our cave, and without warning they zapped us again, and when we came to we were back in the meadow. They had dressed us as well as they could. They had given us back all our equipment. And they had formed their semicircle around us just as they had when we landed.

We did not say good-bye. As fast as we could, we followed Richelieu back into the ship, and — hardly being able to wait to get at our razors — battened down all the hatches and took off.

What was that, Senator? What does all this have to do with my refusing to allow women on First Contact missions?

The answer is *everything*. Hildreth was able to tell us why the puffballs had let us go free. As I said, their emotions were just enough like our own for him to perceive them.

They had let us go free because they were sorry for us. They had concluded that we were awfully unhappy because we refused to breed in captivity.

My God, gentlemen, don't you realize that if we'd had women aboard we'd still *be* there?

10
Mating Season

"Mating Season" was first published in Southwest Review 37 *in the Spring, 1952, issue. This is the story's first appearance in a book.*

Each evening after supper, all the *nice* people who lived at Mrs. Weatherbleak's came down into the parlor for an hour or two. Old Judge Ullbright limped in across the Turkey carpet with his *Law Review* under his arm. Mr. and Mrs. Hiram Puny sat themselves stiffly side by side on the red davenport. George Giele opened the door for Miss Luckmeyer, who taught music at the Junior High School, and followed her over to the bamboo love-seat by the fireplace. Finally, having supervised the clearing of the table, Mrs. Weatherbleak came in herself, smiled at everyone over the faded velvet of her bosom, and signalled to George that the television set could be turned on.

On that first Tuesday in July, though, there was a difference. In the doorway, Mrs. Weatherbleak stopped dead still. Her smile quivered over the custard creases of her face, and set there, pointing its corners at the spots of rouge which, like bobbing buoys, told where her vanished cheekbones lay. She cocked her head to listen in the hall.

The Timeless Tales of Reginald Bretnor

There was no sound except the broken-bellows breathing of the Judge. Something, they knew, was up. This had not happened since poor Mrs. Peterson had passed away, nested among her long-unopened trunks— or, at least, since that odd boy down the street had set the palm on fire.

Mrs. Weatherbleak raised a warning finger. She closed the door silently. She giggled, a dry Tin Woodman sound. "Oh, oh," she said, "you can't imagine it. It's our Miss Visser. She's *engaged*. She told me so herself. She's going to marry Mr. Margolis."

They stirred, expressing their appreciation through the eloquence of creaking oak and leather, and bound bamboo, and horsehair muffled springs.

The Judge coughed thickly, and nodded, and held his spectacles up to his big, veined nose.

Miss Luckmeyer glanced down at her own body, tightly girdled so that it might not betray the schooled severity of her narrow face. It's high time," she said.

Mr. Hiram Puny snickered nervously.

Mrs. Hiram Puny unlocked the fingers of her little hands, and let them clasp her knees, and sniffed. "Live and let live," she addressed the air. "I think it's nice. I think we should do something nice for them, anyway."

George Giele fiddled with the bunch of keys in his vest pocket, and nudged Miss Luckmeyer ever so slightly.

And Mrs. Weatherbleak, savoring these grace notes, crossed the room to her own high-crowned chair, sighed herself into its accustomed valleys, and reached out for her copy of *Lucille*. "I told them to drop in, the both of them. Just for this once, of course— I made that clear. I'm sure it ought to be, well, interesting."

Mating Season

"I think it's very nice of you indeed," said Mrs. Hiram Puny.

Mrs. Weatherbleak opened the book at random on her lap. "I promised her I wouldn't say a word," she giggled. "We'll all pretend it's still a big surprise."

The Judge put on his spectacles. George Giele began to flip the pictured pages of a magazine, holding it over so that Miss Luckmeyer might see. Mrs. Hiram Puny folded her hands again.

Presently there was a knock of knuckles on the door. They all looked up. "Come in, my dear," Mrs. Weatherbleak called. "Come in."

Annette Visser was a tall girl, all angles. Under her short-sleeved sweater, her breasts were like two tangerines, stuck on by a surrealist, too high, too far apart. Her eyes were black and bright. She held her little Mr. Margolis tightly by the hand— at once quite happy, and afraid to be.

Judge Ullbright, gasping, had risen to his feet, and Mr. Hiram Puny was doing so with a squeak of shoes. George Giele had caught himself halfway.

Mrs. Weatherbleak's smile had set. "I am so glad you could come by, just for a minute, dear. Now do sit down." She looked around. "All of us know Miss Visser, I am sure, and Arthur Margolis. And she has something very interesting to tell us, too. Haven't you, dear?"

Annette Visser swallowed. Her too-tight, brownish skin flushed faintly. Jerkily, she edged with Mr. Margolis toward the piano bench. They sat, still holding hands. "Arthur— Arthur and me—" she said in a thin, clear voice. "We're getting married."

"Uh— yeah, that's right," Arthur Margolis, grinning, nodded uncertainly.

There was a moment's silence. Then, "Isn't that *lovely*?" cried Mrs. Weatherbleak. And, "Well, *well*," the Judge coughed, easing himself back into his chair. And Mr. Hiram Puny said, "Congratulations," just as if somebody had sold a fine big piece of real estate.

"How very, very nice!" Mrs. Hiram Puny fluttered her hands. "I'm sure I hope that you'll be very happy–" She peered at them nearsightedly. "–anyway."

George Giele and Miss Luckmeyer said nothing.

"Dear, I hope you'll have a pretty wedding in a church?" inquired Mrs. Weatherbleak.

Annette Visser laughed excitedly. "Not us. We can't spend all that money— apartments cost too much. We'll run down to the City Hall this weekend. It isn't *where* you're married that really counts."

"Oh, goodness no," Mrs. Hiram Puny said, and sighed. "It's just a shame, that's all."

Miss Luckmeyer had been staring at the girl's skin, her dull hair, the length and thinness of her arms and legs. She had observed that Arthur Margolis was spindle-shanked and pale. Now she shut her eyes; and, to George Giele, her narrowing smile at once revealed her thought. He leaned toward her. "Maybe it'll seem completely natural to them," he whispered in her ear.

She started; her smile disappeared. And Mr. Hiram Puny, his hearing still acute, swivelled around and said, "Huh? I don't get it," loudly.

Mrs. Weatherbleak raised her voice across the room. "You do have an apartment?"

Annette Visser hesitated. Though she could not have overheard George Giele, she suddenly seemed ill-

Mating Season

at-ease. "We— we found one out in Chula Vista," she said at last. "It's a long way from where Arthur works. But it is furnished, and it's sort of cute." She turned to him. "We'd better go now, hadn't we?"

"I'm *so* glad you dropped in," Mrs. Weatherbleak said.

Then Arthur Margolis, embarrassed, went around and shook hands with the men, and invited everybody to drop by sometime, and said that he and Nettie had liked living there; it was so much like home.

Finally the door clicked, and they were gone.

Sharply, Mrs. Weatherbleak shut her book. "Well, I *never*. That's gratitude for you. Not even a week's notice!"

"Oh, how we *know*," Mrs. Puny said. "We learned our lesson when Mr. Puny was in real estate."

"What I can't understand—" Shuddering, Miss Luckmeyer let her fingers slide slowly down her thighs. "—is why they'd *want* to? It's— it's indecent."

George Giele's square jaw split in a grin. "Guess it's the mating season— rabbits, birds, seagulls, everything."

The Judge chuckled and coughed. Mr. Puny laughed the way he usually did at Milton Berle. Miss Luckmeyer tittered.

"Well, evolution's very strange," Mrs. Weatherbleak observed. "It makes some people even look peculiar— like pigs and things."

"That's *true*," Mrs. Puny replied. "Take Mildred Camber and that chow of hers. It's almost frightening when you think of it. And if they look like that—" She shivered. "—maybe they have the instincts too. Maybe the poor things can't help themselves."

Miss Luckmeyer leaned forward. "Do bugs have mating seasons?" she asked. "Because that's what both of them remind me of— some kind of bug: brown, with a skinny body and lots of legs. Something I've seen not awfully long ago."

"Stick-insects!" George Giele slapped his knee. "You hit it on the head!"

The Judge guffawed. Hiram Puny snickered. Mrs. Weatherbleak giggled seismically.

"Say, say!" George Giele reached for the picture magazine, opened it, held it up. "They're right in here. Look! Praying mantises. See how much taller she is than he? See, they're mating—"

Mrs. Puny turned delicately away.

"—and afterwards she eats him up—"

He stopped. There was a sudden silence. The idea filled the room. They tasted it.

George Giele's jowls turned red. "*That's* what she'll do!" His laughter soared. "She'll eat him up! With— with salt and pepper. A-a-afterwards!"

"That isn't nice at all," Mrs. Puny quavered. "*Nobody* would do *that*."

Miss Luckmeyer, eyes sparkling, reached for the magazine without a word.

Each evening after supper, all the *nice* people who lived at Mrs. Weatherbleak's came down into the parlor for an hour or so; and, every evening in the parlor, the idea grew. Amusing details of behavior were remembered; newly-found facets of resemblance were discussed...

"It's queer, Mrs. Weatherbleak. It's as George says. She has a *hungry* look." "I know it isn't so— but don't *you* feel that their arms and legs have more joints than they ought to have?" "Hm-m, yes, a colleague on the bench once told me of a case in France, a most unpleasant case..."

As always, too, coincidence brought fresh material to the fantasy. George Giele twice saw Arthur Margolis on a downtown street. "Well," he reported, "honeymoon can't be over. He's still on the menu, ha-ha-ha!"

And, a week after the wedding, Hiram Puny ran into Annette Visser in a chain store, shopping on bargain day, her cart piled high. She had a case of catsup—a whole case. "What'd she want with that, hey?" he asked afterwards. "I don't get it, unless—"

The idea held them, and they nourished it. Each took that tenuous similarity, that cruelly apt abstraction of design, and filled it in. George Giele grinned, talking of knives and forks and condiments. Hiram Puny listened to him, and said, "Yum-yum, crunch-crunch," and snickered. Painting no clear picture of his own, Judge Ullbright cited cases; the Donner Party was his favorite. Mrs. Weatherbleak giggled, and shook her head, and murmured, "I can just see her now."

Miss Luckmeyer, though, showed little interest in the consummation. On these occasions, she closed her eyes, and, with satisfaction, considered the dry, rustling, entomological caresses which must precede it.

For three weeks, the jest thrived. Then, in its fullness, it was screened off, suddenly shrouded, forbidden as a parlor subject of discussion.

One evening, Hiram Puny came down alone, a little worried, a little shamefaced. Mrs. Puny, he said, was having nightmares. He'd told her she was foolish, taking it that way. Wasn't it just a joke, ha-ha? But she'd wake up, all pale as if she was scared to death, and then she'd lie there and swear she could see stick-insects in the wallpaper pattern, fighting, and trying to eat each other up, and— well, doing things.

Swift glances were exchanged, covert reminders that everybody knew of Mrs. Puny's stay in a small private hospital.

She could see the bugs change into Miss Visser and Mr. Margolis, Mr. Puny reported. She couldn't stand it any more.

Mrs. Weatherbleak pursed her lips. She clucked maternally. She frowned at George Giele, who was on the point of saying something tart. "Now, Mr. Puny," she declared, "don't you fret. You tell her I know how sensitive she is, poor dear, and to just come on down. We're going to promise never to bring it up again." She peered at them. "Aren't we?"

George Giele shrugged. The Judge formally gave his word. "Silence is golden," Miss Luckmeyer said, a little acidly.

Some minutes later, Mrs. Puny joined them, and watched the television show. And they kept their promise.

They kept their promise for ten entire days. By then, Arthur Margolis had disappeared.

The policeman was quite young, and fairly handsome in his new brown suit; and Mrs. Weatherbleak, sensing something in the wind, invited him into the parlor.

Mating Season

Supper was over, and everyone was there. The policeman frowned slightly when he saw them. "They all live here?" he asked of Mrs. Weatherbleak.

She said they did, and simpered, and added that they were her dearest friends.

"Okay." He nodded and sat down. "You know an Arthur Margolis?"

Nobody answered. Only the creaking furniture replied.

"Margolis," he repeated. "Arthur. Didn't he use to live here?"

Their glances darted, quickly, like avid flies.

"I *knew* it." Mrs. Hiram Puny's small head pecked the air. "I could tell right from the first that he was—*shady*."

"Mrs. Puny's a real judge of character," agreed her husband. "She spots 'em every time. Why, I remember once—"

Mrs. Weatherbleak broke in loudly. "You'd never think it, not to look at him. If I'd dreamed for a minute—well, he'd not have set foot in this house, believe me!"

"What'd he do, Sergeant?" George Giele asked. "What'd you get him for?"

Woodenly, the policeman looked from face to face. "Not anything, far as I know. The guy's missing, is all."

There was a silence, soft and perilous, hovering there. The tip of Mrs. Weatherbleak's tongue came out to lick her parched cranberry lips. She stared at Mrs. Puny curiously. "*Missing?*" came her dry whisper. "*Really?*"

Since Friday, the policeman said. Yeah. Once a month, maybe, the lumber firm sent Arthur Margolis up to the mill at Julian. He stayed a couple of days, usually, checking accounts. On Friday morning, he told his wife he thought he'd have to go. She didn't even start to worry till Sunday night. Then, Monday, his boss had phoned. Where was Arthur? *Julian*? Heck no, he hadn't even shown up for work on Friday. "So there we are," the policeman said. "It's sure rough on her; she says they're newlyweds." He shook his head. "And the trail's four days cold already."

"Four days?" George Giele exclaimed. "Why that's enough—"

He stopped; and Hiram Puny snickered suddenly. "Yum-yum, crunch-crunch," he cackled, showing his teeth. And then, with a swift, sidelong look at Mrs. Puny, he too was silent.

Miss Luckmeyer looked up, clinical interest shining in her eyes. "You haven't found the body?" she inquired.

There was a hardness in the policeman's face. "What is this?" he demanded. "What's all this 'yum-yum' stuff? Lady, what makes you think there's got to be a body? Maybe you people know something I don't know?"

"Oh, goodness—" Mrs. Weatherbleak's smile, congealing, warned the room. "—it isn't that at all."

"Ha-ha!" George Giele shifted in his seat. "It's just a—sort of a standing joke. Something somebody said—"

They chorused their corroboration.

"Damn' funny," remarked the policeman. "Like a crutch." He paused. "That crack about the body— that's part of it, I guess?"

"No," snapped Miss Luckmeyer. "I mean, if he's not dead— why ever else do people disappear?"

Mating Season

The policeman told her there were other reasons. He took a ball-point pen and a sheaf of filing cards from his pocket, and asked his questions. Did the guy drink? What about other women? Debts? So on and so on.

They answered him as well as they knew how, as well as their preoccupation would permit. Mrs. Puny closed her eyes; swaying a little, fingers kneading her knees, she forced out her responses— pale, fragmentary phrases rendered unreal by the brutality which impaled her mind.

Finally, the policeman left. The thought they shared was free, to live, to flow beyond the tight enclosure of each privacy, to walk into the room.

"It's queer," George Giele said, and shivered. "Damn' queer."

"Yes, isn't it?" Mrs. Weatherbleak replied in a hushed voice. "He was such a *thin* man."

"My God!" Miss Luckmeyer spat. "No one would *really*—"

The Judge sat up. The folded flesh above his collar shook as he spoke. "Ah, wouldn't they? You don't know the world then. There was that Sutting case, just for example— a frightful thing. And—"

Mrs. Puny covered her face. She whimpered through the leanness of her hands. She lurched erect, staggered, ran from the room leaving the door ajar.

Her husband hesitated. He snickered foolishly. Then, as Miss Luckmeyer rose, he found his feet. As they went after Mrs. Puny, he muttered something about "more sleeping pills" over his shoulder.

Mrs. Weatherbleak, Judge Ullbright, and George Giele remained alone.

"She's just too— well, *imaginative*," Mrs. Weatherbleak observed, letting the broad shelf of her bosom rise and fall.

"It doesn't do to close your eyes to things," said the Judge, "but you mustn't let 'em grow on you, either. Mrs. Puny lacks — er — self-control."

"That four day business," declared George Giele, "is enough to give anyone the creeps."

Then the phone rang in the hall; and Mrs. Weatherbleak got up to answer it, promising she'd be right back. In a moment, they heard her voice, metallic, shaping the tones of friendliness without its warmth.

"Oh, yes, Miss Visser— I mean, Mrs. Margolis — yes, we know all about it, you poor dear. ... Yes, the police were here. ... Just asking questions, dear. ... Of course, it must be awful for you there, all by yourself. I can *quite* understand why. ... Well— I don't know. For a few days, you say? ... *Naturally*, just till they find him, dear, and it *is* spoken for. ... No, no, I don't mean you *can't* have it, but—" Mrs. Weatherbleak's voice became more intimate. "—there isn't a single place left in the dining room, dear. I'll have to have your meals all served upstairs. I know you won't mind that."

At first, wrapped in the immediacy of her own concern, Annette Margolis noticed nothing strange. She was glad to have breakfast and supper in her room; she didn't have to talk. She came and went, unconscious of the implications which might have been conveyed by a glance, an attitude, a word. When Mrs. Puny, with a cry, ducked back behind a door at the sight of her, it was coincidence. When Mrs. Weatherbleak gave her a magazine to read, it was an act of simple kindness; she scanned the pages, shivered a little at the mantises, and put the thing aside. She did not wonder what went on each evening in the parlor.

Not at first. Not until the day before the police found Arthur Margolis.

She came in ten minutes late for supper. She looked for Mrs. Weatherbleak to tell her she was back. She found her in the dining room. "Hello," she called.

No one replied. Mrs. Puny's little hand jerked upward to her lips. The others simply stared. No one invited her to enter. Even though there were two vacant seats, nobody said a word.

And she stared too, while Mrs. Weatherbleak's smile assumed its shape to say, "I'll have your supper sent up right away, dear."

Afterwards she thought about it in her room, and slowly the sense of wrongness grew on her, the sense of something horrible carefully veiled. It was persistent. The next day, even before she heard that Arthur had been found, even as she was packing her grip to go, it haunted her.

That evening, after supper, all the nice people who lived at Mrs. Weatherbleak's came down into the parlor to hear the news. Even Mrs. Puny came, light-headed in her sudden convalescence. They took their places, and, exchanging speculations on how and where and why, they waited eagerly.

Mrs. Weatherbleak entered. She stood dead still until the custard creases of her smile had set. Cocking her head, she listened in the hall. She closed the door.

"Our Mrs. Margolis—" Her sharp, dry giggle welled; her surface shook. "She's upstairs packing now. She told me— everything."

"Where did they find him?" Miss Luckmeyer asked impatiently. The others echoed her.

But Mrs. Weatherbleak, before she answered, minced tantalizingly across the room to her own chair, sat there, regarded them. Again, she giggled. "Well," she began, "it's just the funniest thing. They didn't really find him. He found himself."

"Not in a casserole?" George Giele cried, in mock astonishment. And they all laughed.

"No, in Los Angeles," Mrs. Weatherbleak said. "He walked into one of those offices— is it called Travellers' Aid? — and told them that he'd just remembered who he was. He said he'd had a fall, or maybe a car had hit him — he wasn't sure which — and that he'd been sort of wandering for those four days."

"I'll *bet*," Hiram Puny remarked sarcastically.

"I'll bet he caught on when she shook catsup on him!" George Giele roared. "Oh, ha-ha-ha! I'll bet the male mantis tries to get away— and then his instincts bring him back." He opened his arms wide. "Come to my mandibles, you pretty thing," he cooed seductively.

"He-he-he-he-he-heee!" squealed Mrs. Puny. "Come to my man-di-bles!"

"Yum-yum," her husband snickered, "crunch-crunch."

They filled the room with laughter. George Giele's neck turned red. The Judge coughed apoplectically. And then, abruptly, they saw the open door.

Annette Margolis stood there, holding her overnight bag in one thin hand. Curiously, she no longer resembled a stick-insect. Her face was twisted, and her black eyes blazed. She looked only like a furious woman, outraged.

Mating Season

There was no sound except the broken-bellows breathing of the Judge. For seconds, there was no sound.

The tall girl's lips drew back against her teeth. Her voice was harsh and barely audible. "You— *you filthy things!*" she said.

And that was all. The hall was empty.

They heard the front door bang; they heard swift running steps.

Slowly, Mrs. Weatherbleak's smile collapsed. She rose. "*Eavesdropping!*" she exclaimed. "After all I've done for her. After I let her have that room. I'll never let *her* in this house again, you can be sure!"

"My God, couldn't she see that it was just a joke?" George Giele asked.

Mrs. Puny fluttered her hands. "I don't think she was *at all* nice," she said.

Then Mrs. Weatherbleak went to the door, and shut it firmly so that no one might intrude upon their privacy.

11
Mrs. Pigafetta Swims Well

The publishing history of "Mrs. Pigafetta Swims Well" started out modestly enough in October, 1959, with its inclusion in the Peninsula Spectator. *It wasn't printed in the* Magazine of Fantasy and Science Fiction *until May, 1963. Next it appeared in* The 9th Annual Edition of the Year's Best Science Fiction, *edited by Judith Merril and published in hardcover by Simon & Schuster, New York. The same book was brought out in a paperback edition by Dell Publishing, New York, in 1965, by Mayflower-Dell, London, in 1967, and by Mayflower, London, in 1970. Sixteen years later the story appeared once again, this time in a book called* Mermaids!, *edited by Jack Dann and Gardner Dozois, published by Ace Fantasy Books, 1986.*

M r. Coastguard, this is what has happened to Pietro Pugliese, who is captain of the fishing boat *Il Trovatore*, of Monterey. Me, Joe Tonelli, I am his engineer. I know.

It is because of Mrs. Pigafetta, from Taranto. It is her fault. Also the porpoises. It is also because Pietro has been famous—

You do not know? You have not heard how one time he is the great *tenore*? Yes, in Rome, Naples, Venice— even in La Scala in Milano. *Do, re, mi, fa*—like so, only with more beauty. Caruso, Gigli—those fellows can only make a squeak alongside Pietro, I tell you.

Mrs. Pigafetta Swims Well

So what, you say? It is important. It is why Mrs. Pigafetta becomes his landlady. It is why she hides his clothes so that he cannot run away like her first husband who maybe is in Boston. It is why the porpoises—

Okay, Mr. Coastguard, okay. I will tell one thing at one time. I will begin when first I hear Pietro sing, last Tuesday night.

He calls to me when he is at the wheel. Our hold is full of fish. The sea is smooth. The moon hangs in the sky like a fine oyster. But I can see that he is still not happy. He has not been happy for two months. All the time he shakes his head. He sighs.

I am worried. I ask if maybe he has a bad stomach, but he does not reply. All at once, his head is thrown back—his mouth is open—he sings! It is from the last act of *Tosca*, in the jail. They are going to execute this guy, and he is singing good-bye to the soprano, who is his girl. You know? That is why it is sad.

I am full of surprise. Never have I heard a voice so rich—like the best *zabaglione*, made with egg yolk, sugar, sweet wine. Also it is strong, like a good foghorn. Even the mast trembles.

I listen to the end. I look at him. His face is to the moon. He weeps! Slowly, many tears roll down his cheeks. What would you do? I want him to feel good. I tell him he is great. I cry, *Bravissimo!*

At last he speaks, as from the grave. "Joe, it is as you say. It is true I am a great man. Even the angels do not have a voice like me. And now"—his chest goes up and down—"it is this voice which cooks my goose! Almost, I lose all hope. But I say, 'Joe is my good friend. Maybe he can help—'"

Then, Mr. Coastguard, I hear the story. His papa is a fisherman. Once, they come to Naples. While Pietro mends the nets, he sings. He is young, handsome. A rich *marchesa* hears him. And it is done! A year—the world is at his feet. He has a palace, a gold watch, mistresses—yes, *principessas*, girls from the ballet, the wives of millionaires! He sings. All—kings, queens, cardinals—they cry with joy. Even the English often clap their hands.

He is innocent. He does not know the other singers burn with jealousy. He does not know the critics envy him. They plot. Always they say bad things. One day there is no place for him to sing! Ah, he is wounded to the heart. He goes away. He takes a cabin on a little ship. For two days, without a fee, he sings to the waves, the passengers, the crew. But he is betrayed! The sea has envy too. There comes a storm. Those people on the ship are stupid fools. They say it is his fault. They—they throw him overboard!

He tells me this. Again he sighs. "I cannot swim. I fight against the waves. I call aloud the names of many saints. I sink! But I am not afraid. When I come up, I sing! Again the water swallows me. Then—all is black. My friend, when I awake I think that I am dead. But I am not. I am in Mrs. Pigafetta's house."

Mr. Coastguard, it is a miracle! The ship is near Taranto. There is this island. And on it is the *penzione* of Mrs. Pigafetta, for shipwrecked sailors. She has heard the fine voice of Pietro in the storm. She has rescued him. It is nothing for Mrs. Pigafetta. She swims well.

He wakes—and she is sitting there, all wet. He is surprised to see her. He makes the sign of the cross, but she says nothing. There is love in her eyes.

Mrs. Pigafetta Swims Well

And she is beautiful! Not thin, like a young girl, but plump and strong, with fine hips—wide like so. Her lips are red. Her hair is black, done up on top. It shines like it has olive oil on it. Besides, she is a woman of experience—

Still, when Pietro tells me this, he grinds his teeth. "Why do I stay with her, my friend? It is because at first I am in love. It is a madness. All night, all day—such passion. There are two sailors there, Greeks; she does not speak to them. Each month she makes them pay. But me—one month, two months, three—I get no bill. She teaches me to swim. We sit on the rocks in the sun, and we sing to each other—*La Forza del Destino, Pagliacci, Rigoletto*. My love has made me deaf. I do not notice that her contralto has the sound of brass. Imagine it!"

Then, in one moment, Pietro's eyes are opened. A day comes when Mrs. Pigafetta pushes him away. She lets him kiss her neck, her ear—that is all! He does not understand. He asks, "*Carissima*, my sweet lobster, what is wrong?"

She pushes him some more. She makes her lips thin. She says, "No, no, Pietro *mio!* We must marry in the Church."

Even as Pietro tells me this, his face is sad. "At once, all is changed. It comes to me that her voice is loud, of poor quality. Besides, I am Pietro Pugliese—there is my public. I must not stay always with one woman. I make a long face. I ask about her first husband, Pigafetta. I ask her, 'He is dead?' And she laughs at me. She shrugs. 'He is in Boston. It is the same.'"

From the wheelhouse of *Il Trovatore*, Pietro looks to port, to starboard. There is light from the moon on the waves. All over, porpoises are playing—

"Ah, she is stubborn! She makes me afraid. I see I have a great problem, with much trouble. Why? You ask me why? Joe, I have one more reason I cannot marry Mrs. Pigafetta in the Church. It is because—"

He moves his hand to show me. His voice shakes.

"—because Mrs. Pigafetta is a woman only from here up. From here down, she is a fish!"

Okay, Mr. Coastguard, you do not believe. It is because, like me, you have never seen a woman like Mrs. Pigafetta. A mermaid? That is what I ask Pietro. He says no, that it is different. Mrs. Pigafetta is a woman of experience—

The days pass. Always she pushes him away. Always she says, "No, we must marry in the Church."

He argues. "If we are married, sometime we have a son. You think I want my son to be a sturgeon, a big sea-bass, perhaps a flounder? I do not know your family."

She laughs. She tells him this cannot be. She says, "Our son can be a bosun in the navy, no worse. Even so, he must know his papa. That is why I push you away."

Soon Pietro tries to escape. He sees a sailing boat. He shouts at it, and runs along the shore. After that, Mrs. Pigafetta takes his clothes. She hides them in her house, which is made in a large cave in the rocks.

But he is brave. Twice more he tries. He swims at night. Each time, the porpoises swim with him. They turn him back, like dogs with a sheep. They are her friends.

When he tells this, he shakes his fist at the porpoises in the sea. "That is when I know that I must be more smart than Mrs. Pigafetta. Again, I sing to her. I praise her voice. And all the time I watch. Ah, she is vain! Two, three times a day she puts on her best hat. She sits at her mirror. She looks at herself one way, then another. She smiles. It is a large hat, with many feathers, much fruit on the top."

Mr. Coastguard, you ask why does she want a hat? But why not? Where she puts the hat she is a woman, not a fish.

Okay, Pietro makes a plan. He promises that they will marry in the Church. After that, she does not say, "No, no." She does not push. But every time she asks when they will marry, he delays.

"*Now?* My pretty perch, my sea anemone! It is the tourist season. You will be kidnaped for your lovely silver tail—sold in the black market to rich Americans!"

For weeks it is like that. At last she loses patience. "You say we go to Rome. You promise a cathedral. You even tell me I will meet this Rossellini. *Bah!* Tomorrow you will swim with me to Taranto. The priest will marry us." She is very angry. "You say it is not safe. All right! There is a church by the water. I will bring a long dress. I will wear perfume. No one will know."

Pietro pretends that he is pleased. He kisses her. Then he looks sad. "But, *cara mia*, there is—there is one small thing." He points at it. "You cannot possibly be married in this hat."

She weeps. She tells him if he loved her he would like her hat.

He kisses her again. He protests his love. It is only that the hat is out of fashion. The women in the town will laugh at her. Besides, the sea has spoiled it. Then he tells his plan. They will swim together, but she will wait for him in the water. He will buy her a new hat.

"Joe, I am smart," Pietro says. "I know that she is mad with love. In the morning, we swim to Taranto. She gives me back my clothes. I put them on. I leave her in the water. Quickly, I take a train. Then I come to America. I buy this boat, *Il Trovatore*. I make an oath—"

Again the tears fall. "My friend, I know that if I keep this oath I will be safe. Four years, I do not sing. Then, two months ago, you go to visit your papa. While you are gone, I bring a lady on the boat. Ah, she is beautiful—the wife of an old man who has a bank. She gives me wine. And—and for one moment I forget! I sing for her. From *Don Giovanni*, from *La Traviata*. But suddenly she points her finger at the sea. I look—and my heart is dead! I see the porpoises. They, too, are listening!"

That is why there has been a sadness on Pietro's soul. The porpoises are Mrs. Pigafetta's friends. He knows that they will tell her where he is.

I say, "Have courage! Taranto is a long way. The porpoises will not want to go so far. It will take many months for her to come."

His tears fall like rain. "No, no." he cries. "The porpoises shout to each other through the sea. Also, there is the Panama Canal. She swims well. She will be here soon!"

Mr. Coastguard, the sea is full of porpoises. They play. They leap into the air. There are more now. Also they seem more glad.

"Joe, look!" Pietro grabs my arm. "That is how they are when she is near. I tell you, she comes tonight! You must help me, Joe!"

I say to him, "Have no fear. I do not let her take you back. I will do what you want."

Mrs. Pigafetta Swims Well

He embraces me. He says: "I have a plan. Maybe once more I can be more smart than Mrs. Pigafetta. You remember one week ago, when we are in San Pedro, I go ashore? Okay, I go to buy a hat. It is a fine hat, the new style, green, with bright things that hang down and a long plume from the top."

The box is in the wheelhouse. He opens it. "I have paid eighteen dollars. Maybe when you give her this fine hat she is shamed and will go away."

"*Me?*" I say.

"Yes, yes! We watch the porpoises so I can tell when she has come real close. We bring Nick from the galley to hold the wheel. You tie me to the mast—"

I ask, "Why must I tie you to the mast?"

He looks over his shoulder. He makes his voice low. "Because it is a smart trick, made by a Greek. You tie me to the mast with lots of rope, good and strong. You wait on deck. She calls out from the sea, Pietro *mio*, where are you? I sing a little bit. She comes more quickly. She grabs the rail. She wants to climb aboard—Joe, that is when you must think well! You must say, 'Mrs. Pigafetta, it is nice meeting you. Pietro has bought for you this hat. It is expensive. It is a token of his love. But he cannot go with you to your house.' Then you must tell her something so she goes away."

For two hours, we talk about what I must tell to Mrs. Pigafetta. Sometimes Pietro weeps. Sometimes he is angry. But at last I get a good thought. I say, "I will tell her that I tie you up because you are crazy in the head with love—that you try to jump into the sea—that you believe a fat porpoise is Mrs. Pigafetta."

It is now very late. The moon has fallen in the sky. There are more porpoises even than before. They swim around *Il Trovatore*. All the time, they look at us.

Suddenly, Pietro starts to tremble. He whispers, "*She is near!*" He crouches by the mast. We call for Nick to hold the wheel. I take the rope—

And then—crash! bang!—something hits *Il Trovatore* a great blow on the bottom. The stern lifts in the air. I fall. Pietro cries aloud.

What is it? A great fish? A whale? I do not know. Next thing, I hear my engine. It runs fast—faster, faster! It screams—

I forget Pietro! I forget all but my engine. I go to it like a mama to her child who is hurt. Nick is there too. He shouts, "What is wrong?" I shout back, "A fish has broken the propeller!" I turn the engine off.

We look to see if there is a bad leak. Maybe for five minutes we look. Then, all at once—I remember! We leap up to the deck—

The boat has stopped in the water. It rocks gently. All is still. The porpoises have gone. I guess the big fish has gone too. And Pietro? He is not there anymore.

Across the deck, there is sea water. In a strip—wide like so—it is wet. Also, on the deck there is the box. Next to it is a hat. But, Mr. Coastguard, it is not the fine hat Pietro buys down in San Pedro. Here, look at it! See how it is out of fashion? See the flowers, the fruit? See how it has been spoiled by the sea?

Ah, when we see it, we are just like you. At first we have no words. Then, to port, to starboard, we shout loudly, "Pietro! Where are you, Pietro? Answer us! Come back!"

Mrs. Pigafetta Swims Well

There is no answer. Only, far away, we hear this voice singing. It is strong and full of joy. But it is not Pietro's voice. It is a contralto—with the sound of brass.

No, Mr. Coastguard, I do not think that you will find Pietro. It is too late. Mrs. Pigafetta is a woman of experience. She swims well.

12
The Murderers' Circle

"The Murderers' Circle"' was first published in Ellery Queen's Mystery Magazine *in July, 1988. This is the story's first appearance in a book.*

The invitation came as almost a complete surprise to Bryce Lasher, not because he didn't think he deserved it — he knew he did — but because, after making his abrasive reputation as a mystery critic by denigrating the traditional British detective novel and excoriating its writers, he had expected nothing but enmity on his arrival in London, and for nine days that was exactly what he had experienced — that and, of course, often being snubbed completely, which was even more gratifying.

His publisher, who had made money out of the UK and Commonwealth rights to his three ruthless, overly explicit novels (termed mysteries only because no one could deny they were full of murders), had at first offered him consolation. "Don't worry, laddie," he'd said. "They're just jealous of your sales in Liverpool." Then he had realized that no consolation was necessary.

But even Sounders Egan, the company's editor-in-chief — a neat, military little man, who had negotiated Lasher's very favorable contracts — though he was invariably polite and solicitous, could not quite conceal his own suppressed antagonism. He did his duty, arrang-

The Murderers' Circle

ing autographing parties and bashes for fellow writers, critics and reviewers (which were attended mostly by those who needed the free drinks), and even two speaking engagements, one of them at some sort of police training school where his audience appeared rather puzzled. When the critics and reviewers labelled Lasher abusive, unintelligent, and semiliterate, Egan actually seemed to delight in handing him the clippings. Therefore Lasher was astonished when Egan himself extended the invitation.

The business day had almost ended. Lasher had happily signed a satisfying contract for a fourth novel not yet written, and they had had a drink to cement the deal. He had actually risen to take off when Egan put a friendly arm around his shoulders and said, as though it were a sudden inspiration, "Bryce — you don't mind if I call you Bryce, do you? — do you have anything planned for this evening?"

Lasher had promised himself to spend the evening prowling Soho, where he suspected that his personal decor, patterned after the most expensive male ads in *Vanity Fair*, would bring him a variety of interesting adventures, but he quickly decided that it would keep. *Well, well!* he thought. *Are they starting to come around? Or are they going to try to soft-soap me into laying off?* He laughed to himself. If they thought they'd stop him that way, they'd better have another think coming.

"I guess I don't," he answered. "What's up?"

"Well, I don't know if this'll interest you," said Egan, "but a small group of us meet about once a month and have dinner, and sometimes we have a speaker but sometimes we just talk things over. Some of us are authors—there's Dame Euridice Claythorpe, for example —"

Woof! thought Lasher. Dame Euridice, with more than 130 novels to her credit, was the unchallenged *doyenne* of country house party mysteries; much of what he had said about her work would, in a stricter age, have been considered absolutely libelous.

"She and who else?"

"Oh, there'll be other writers, and a critic or two, naturally, and Commissioner Thwaites-Horton — you know, he runs Scotland Yard. Some of us are into the book end; others are *aficionados* — really avid ones too. But Jennifer Ouseley'll be here any minute now. She's driving right down, so you might like to ride with her. She'll fill you in on the others."

Jennifer Ouseley had come to be regarded as Dame Euridice's foremost amanuensis and natural successor, and the comments Lasher had made on her work had been tempered only by his realization that, of all mystery writers, she was without doubt the most desirable, at least physically. Not only had she been featured in the tabloids caparisoned only in an infinitesimal French bikini, but thousands of British housewives daydreamed of her reputedly tempestuous love affairs. She had black hair, full red lips, a Gypsy's eyes. The idea of riding down there with her — wherever *there* might be — made Lasher surreptitiously lick his lips.

"And you won't have to bother to dress," Egan went on. "We're very informal — a tight little group, all very close friends, quite democratic really. After all, Peter Splain was a Yarmouth fishing smack captain for years before he took up writing, and Braxton Bellingham — remember, those very technical mysteries? — is scarcely a public school man, even if he is one of our foremost authorities on water snails. Then there's our

The Murderers' Circle

host for the evening, dear old Alf Hobble — a real diamond in the rough and rich as Croesus. But hold on — here's Jennifer now—"

The door had opened, and there she was. Her eyes swept over Lasher, doing all sorts of things to his glands. She smiled.

"And who have we here, Sandy?" she asked.

"My dear," Egan replied, "this is Bryce Lasher, of whom you've certainly heard—"

Licking his chops, and not surreptitiously, Lasher wondered momentarily about how she'd react. He needn't have. Her smile embraced him. She laughed softly. "Of *course!*" she cried out. "Why, what *fun!*"

"I told Bryce he could ride down with you," Egan said. "I was sure you wouldn't mind."

She laughed again. "Not if he doesn't."

Lasher indicated he didn't mind a bit.

"Well, let's get started then," she said, taking his arm. "We have to get through all the traffic and then it's a good twenty miles. You'll want to get there in time for cocktails and have a chance to meet everybody."

Egan saw them to her car, a Daimler Sovereign, and she swept expertly out into the traffic.

"Where are we headed?" Lasher asked.

"Didn't Sandy tell you? Alfie Hobble has an estate out near Warhampton, a regular baronial affair — or rather what some Victorian get-rich-quick thought was baronial. He's a fine host, and we often meet there."

"And who's we? Egan mentioned Dame Euridice and a few others, but then you arrived."

"We call ourselves The Murderer's Circle. There's Aston Tourneau, the publisher, and Lacey Morland, Alfie's daughter, who thinks she's a *femme fatale* because she's been divorced three times, and sweet old Marina Federescu, who's a baroness and who really was a *femme fatale* — a spy for both sides in World War I, imagine it! But you'll meet them all presently. Did you know I'm starting a new novel? It's about three or four murders at a sort of super house party at a ski lodge near Aspen — that's in your state of Colorado, isn't it?"

Lasher replied that indeed it was; he knew the area well; he had skied there many times. *The Murderers' Circle!* he thought. *Don't these Brits even suspect how far off the beam they are with their pretty little house party set-ups? And now she wants to inflict that sort of garbage on Colorado!* But when she started to ask him questions about American police procedure he managed to answer all of them while keeping a straight face.

She drove fast and expertly, and once they had the worst traffic behind them the miles flew swiftly even after they left the main artery for a winding country road. Finally she braked, turning in between two great stone and iron gates.

"Here we are," she told him. "Hobble Manor. Cozy, isn't it?"

He beheld an enormous stone pile, grimly turreted but in no discernible style.

A bald and massive butler stood at the door to greet them. A huge Irish footman who looked as though he might have survived some years of IRA bomb-throwing came out to take the car.

"Good evening, Gudgins," said Miss Ouseley. "I've brought our guest, Mr. Bryce Lasher."

"Good evening, sir," rumbled Gudgins. "Mr. Hobble is awaiting you. If you and Miss Ouseley will come with me?"

The Murderers' Circle

They followed him into a large room where the members of The Murderers' Circle were chatting happily and busily drinking. Egan, surprisingly there ahead of them, made the introductions: Alf Hobble, dressed expensively but in poor taste; his daughter, much as she had been described; the aged Baroness, busy with a huge martini; His Grace, the Bishop of Thaxeter, bluff and florid, who looked as though he probably rode to hounds; Braxton Bellingham, thin and dehydrated; Peter Splain in rough tweeds, puffing a malodorous pipe; and the others whom Egan had already mentioned. Lasher was impressed by none of them, not even by Commissioner Thwaites-Horton, whom he had pictured as a ramrod-straight, sternly martial type, but who turned out to be a bit overweight, blue-eyed and rosy-cheeked, and definitely Churchillian in outline. The only ones who looked at him as though he had been left too long out of the fridge were a Captain Something-or-other of one of the Guards regiments and his drawn, hawk-eyed wife.

Even the Commissioner went out of his way to make Lasher welcome, remarking jocularly that after all it was murder that united them, so that difference of opinion really ought not to be allowed to spoil their fun, and Lasher for once obligingly agreed, telling himself that they really were out to butter him up.

He had one drink — the Scotch was superb — and a second and a third, taking part in some of the small talk, and wondering when would be the best time to activate the mini-recorder he always had with him when discussing contracts.

Presently, they trooped into the dining room, having been summoned by yet another large Irish footman, and Lasher was seated in the place of honor between the Commissioner, who apparently was to preside, and the aged Dame Euridice, who chattered away about *la haute cuisine*, fine wines, and the difficulty one had in finding servants nowadays. "After all, Mr. Lasher," she sighed, "we can't all have the luck of Alfred there and find someone as talented as Gudgins, can we?"

The wines were excellent, the food had been prepared by a master chef, and the two footmen had been well trained. Lasher found himself actually glowing, and he started composing, in his mind, the cutting phrases which would tell The Murderers' Circle what he thought of it and of its absurdly dated novels. The talk flowed through him and around him until the last dessert had been praised and finished and the footmen were preparing to serve coffee and liqueurs.

Then the Commissioner stood, held up an admonitory hand for silence, and called the meeting to order.

"It is our good fortune this evening," he began, "to have with us the very well-known novelist and mystery critic, Mr. Bryce Lasher, with whose work we are all familiar." He beamed down at Lasher, who had flipped on his recorder. "I for one must say that I'm delighted to have him here in our midst."

The Baroness Marina Federescu emitted a throaty chuckle, and Alfred Hobble politely said, "'Ear, 'ear!"

"Indeed yes," the Commissioner continued, "and I'm sure that our guest will not feel that I'm imposing if I ask him to say a few words about the subject in which we're all so deeply interested." He looked down again and saw Lasher already rising to his feet. "Thank you," the Commissioner said. "My fellow members, may I present Bryce Lasher."

The Murderers' Circle

Commissioner Thwaites-Horton sat down as Lasher stood to polite applause.

Lasher looked them over. "This isn't going to take long," he said. "All I'm going to tell you is what's wrong with you and your whole picture. For Christ's sake, don't you know Sherlock Holmes is dead? That Poirot and Appleby and all your other so-called great detectives are about as real as Mickey Mouse? Look at your country. My God, you turn out more crap about murder than anybody— and in the whole place you hardly have fifty murders a year! *Fifty* — Christ! — that's less than any small town in the USA."

Forgetting his promise to be terse, he went on in this vein for the better part of fifteen minutes, informing them that they knew nothing about murder, and citing several works by those present to prove his point. Finally, "Let me close this with a bit of good advice," he said. "Can it. Quit writing about something none of you know anything about. Go back to scribbling *Alice in Wonderland* and *Peter Pan*. That's all."

He sat down, again to polite applause, and again the Commissioner arose. Gravely, he looked down at Lasher.

"Thank you, Mr. Lasher," he began. "Of course, all of us here were already familiar with your opinion of the British murder mystery, but it was well to hear it directly and without any of the restraints imposed by literary convention. Therefore I now shall take the liberty — which I'm sure you will not grudge me — of explaining to you how wrong you are."

Lasher snorted.

"You see," continued Thwaites-Horton, "while we British cannot claim to have invented the detective story, we have done more to nourish and develop it than any other people. In no country has the traditional murder mystery been so popular and over so many years. The traditional form has been an addiction comparable to, let us say, the supermarket tabloid in your own land. This became obvious as soon as the Sherlock Holmes stories started to appear, and it grew constantly over the years. At first its social effects were not obvious, and it wasn't really until after the First World War that we, at Scotland Yard, began to suspect what had been going on. Why? My dear Mr. Lasher, it was because of our *falling* murder rate. As you pointed out, we do not have many more than half a hundred murders a year, and this has persisted despite our increasing population. We noticed it, of course, but by the time we really understood what was going on it was too late."

He smiled at Lasher.

"You see, we were getting case after case of what we knew *had to be* murder, case after case where all the ingredients — motive, opportunity, and so on — were present, but where it was impossible to tie the thing together. Poisoning? The poison couldn't be identified. Blunt instrument? The instrument could not be found. Or the corpse was found where it never should have been. Or neither the instrument nor anything else significant could be linked to the obviously guilty suspect. At length — and believe me only after much soul-searching — we reached the inescapable conclusion. Our murder rate had *not* declined. More murders than ever were being committed here in Great Britain — but, Mr. Lasher, *they were perfect murders*. Our traditional detective novels had so trained our murdering public that they were now treating the whole thing as an art. Consider, just

The Murderers' Circle

the novels of dear Dame Euridice are a compendium of every mistake a murderer shouldn't make. We were faced with an insoluble problem."

"You don't expect me to swallow *that*, do you?" sneered Lasher. "So what did you do then? You sure as hell didn't all up and resign!"

"Certainly not. We simply recognized that murder, once so crude a business, was now being practiced as an art and that we would — discreetly of course — have to make the best of it. As I believe you say in the States, 'If you can't lick 'em, join 'em.' That is the reason some of us founded The Murderers' Circle."

"Honest to God! Do you expect me to *believe* that hogwash?" Lasher pushed his chair back roughly. "Well, listen! I wasn't born yesterday, and I'm not buying any of it. But—" he grinned triumphantly. "—you've given me lots of nice hot material good for about twenty columns, and you aren't going to be able to deny any of it." He tapped his pocket. "I've got it all on tape."

"Oh, that doesn't worry us—"

Suddenly Lasher realized that the members of The Murderers' Circle — including the ravishing Miss Ouseley — were watching him very, very intently.

"My dear fellow, I wasn't trying to persuade you. I explained the situation to you simply because we felt that under the circumstances we owed it to you. But you certainly don't worry us."

Again, the Commissioner smiled benignly.

"After all," he said, "nobody is ever going to know that you were here."

13
Paper Tiger

"Paper Tiger" was first published in Ellery Queen's Mystery Magazine 53 *in May, 1969. In 1970 the story appeared in the book* Ellery Queen's Grand Slam, *published in hardcover by both the World Publishing Company, Cleveland, and Nelson, Foster & Scott, Toronto. This book was also issued as a paperback by the Popular Library, New York. Almost two decades later the story was printed once again, this time in* Crimes: My Favorite Mystery Stories, *edited by Elliott Roosevelt, published in cloth by St. Martin's Press, New York.*

Loring Giroux was the direct opposite of Marshal Feng Teh-chih. There was nothing spectacular about him. He had not won the Presidency of the United States by ruthlessly exterminating all his rivals. He had not even campaigned for it dramatically at a time of crisis. He had inherited it. He had been a compromise Vice President, chosen for his Southern votes and as a solid, stable counterweight to the flamboyance of Cardey Corcoran.

Then, two months after taking office, to the sorrow of the ladies and the relief of many high-placed people in his own administration, Cardey had crashed his private plane into a mountainside, taking half his Cabinet and several Secret Service men along with him, and Loring Giroux had moved quietly, with his wife and one unmarried daughter, his shaggy sheepdog and his yellow cat, into the loneliest house in the world.

Paper Tiger

That was when Marshal Feng Teh-chih had started in on him.

Loring Giroux's background was as quiet and solid as his person. He had been a naval officer, a junior deck officer aboard high-tech tankers. He had a decoration or two, awarded after forgotten actions in which nothing much had happened to his ship. He had served in the Louisiana State Legislature. He had been appointed to a board or two in Washington, to something in the Organization of American States, then to a South American ambassadorship. In between, he had practiced law at home. Finally, he had been elected Governor, and then — to everyone's surprise — Vice President.

His ancestry went back before the Louisiana Purchase on the one hand, and to the Revolution on the other. His grandfather had finished up the Civil War as a young captain under Jubal Early; afterwards he had wandered angrily into the West and Mexico, finally returning to a late marriage and a reconciliation with his country. His father had gone to West Point, and had retired, a colonel. He himself was neither short nor tall, fat nor thin. His main distinguishing feature was a slightly Teddy Rooseveltish moustache, which the political cartoonists — Chinese and American alike — at once latched onto.

They also (and the Chinese especially, because they had been ordered to) went for the big striped yellow tomcat. American cartoonists, even the opposition, were almost kind about it; they loved to show Giroux asking the cat's advice on how to catch the mice of international politics, or how he could turn himself into Cardey Corcoran. But the Chinese used it to plug their ancient paper tiger theme. Loring Giroux, they screamed, had brought Beauregard to the White House to prove that the American paper tiger wasn't made of paper after all. The Chinese madness had made lots of headway since the days of Mao Tse-tung and his Red Guards, and Marshal Feng, a Red Guard graduate, had turned it to his private purposes.

Feng concentrated on President Giroux. The Russians now were seldom named, and then only as Giroux's criminal, treacherous, and unspeakable collaborators. Giroux was a weakling. Giroux was the degenerate symbol of a decadent bourgeois society. The missiles, the fusion weapons, which he as President controlled — these were the paper tiger. The young and vigorous Maoist Workers' State, wielding its unconquerable weapon — the thought of Mao and of Feng Teh-chih (though Mao was fading rather rapidly) — would triumph certainly, because survival was the natural prize awarded to the fittest.

"The fittest would survive!" cried Marshal Feng. It was a curious Marxist Darwinism, naive, grossly oversimplified, trumpeted out with each new insult, each new provocation. It accompanied the overrunning of Nepal. It became even more personal and more strident when Feng launched his invasion of North India, penetrating deep into Assam.

It was ridiculous. The press of the Free World thought so, and laughed about it several days a week. The State Department thought it was absurd; so did the Joint Chiefs of Staff. Every Security Council meeting included a few moments of innocent merriment focussed on it.

Until, that is, the Council met on the 16th of September. It was a crash session, with the Joint Chiefs in attendance. Marshal Feng had gone on the air that morning, and President Giroux opened the meeting five-and-a-half hours later. He looked around at the faces, the uniforms, the business suits.

"Gentlemen," he said, "I know that you all either have watched Feng's latest performance or else heard about it. Still, we're going to replay it, so there'll be no misunderstanding."

"Mr. President," exclaimed the Secretary of Defense, "Feng's just a crazy thug. Aren't you taking his nonsense a little seriously?"

"A little, Jake. It isn't every day a man gets this kind of invitation. Let's watch our boy again."

He gestured them to silence; picked up translation headphones but didn't put them on immediately. Feng appeared without warning on the screen, a tall, long-faced North Chinese with basalt eyes. He was lean and hard, an obvious athlete. Giroux turned Feng's speech on suddenly, full blast, like turning on a fire siren.

"Who does he remind you of?" asked the President, unsmiling — knowing that no reply was necessary, that despite the difference of race, language, doctrine, the image of Hitler came instantly to every mind. The speech was Feng's usual one, a screaming rodomontade using all the old clichés, but this time, after barely fifteen minutes, coming to a very different climax.

"You are a filthy Capitalist coward, Loring Giroux. You are afraid of me and of the irresistible thought of Mao Tse-tung. You are afraid because the working masses and their leaders do not fear your paper tiger. We spit on you, Giroux! You are not fit to survive. I will destroy your vile imperialism. I will humiliate you. I, Feng Teh-chih — I myself will rub your face in filth.

Coward! You are afraid to fight. I challenge you to fight, to fight *me*, with your hands, with guns, with knives, anywhere, at any time, with any weapons you desire! Do you understand? Do you dare to fight me, Feng Teh-chih, before the world? No, you do not. You know that you could not survive, corrupt weakling! I will show you how I will destroy you, paper tiger—"

On the screen, an aide stepped into view, carrying a striped orange cat — a cat as much like Beauregard as possible. Feng's left hand grasped it, lifted it. Then, with a swift and brutal judo chop, he broke its back. He hurled the poor small body against a wall, showed all his teeth, and screamed, "*That* is how I will kill you, weak Giroux!"

The screen went blank. The show was over. There was silence. Such a display was difficult for men used to the normal courses of diplomacy to understand. Even the Joint Chiefs, men of war, still could not quite believe what they had seen. Had it not been a replay, their reaction would have been immediate. As it was, they hesitated, looked at the President questioningly, began to simmer as the pressure rose.

Before it could erupt, he touched them with his voice. It was not harsh. It was not cold. But it was quiet as cold steel. "Don't," he said. "Don't comment. That's not the purpose of this get-together."

State looked at CIA, CIA at Defense; the Joint Chiefs exchanged anxious glances.

"You are here for one reason and one reason only–" Loring Giroux rose. "—to hear my decision regarding Marshal Feng's proposal. I have accepted it."

There are things which never should be dropped: rare porcelains, pots of molten lead, live hand grenades. People react too naturally. Instantly noise erupted. *But*

Paper Tiger

it's illegal for a Presi... Constitu... Without any consultation!... B-but we're a civilized peo...

Loring Giroux looked at Quinton, Army, who was sounding off as loudly as the rest. "*General Quinton!*"

Quinton stood, large and dark and graying. He put his palms flat down on the shining table, letting his jaw and football shoulders jut out over it. The others quieted.

"Mr. President," boomed Quinton. "You've flipped. You, sir, are out of your ever-loving mind."

"Why?" rapped Giroux.

"Because, goddammit, you're 61 years old. You're in no shape to fight him hand to hand. Even when we were kids, you couldn't learn to shoot for sour apples. Feng's in top condition. There's not a weapon he's not expert in. You're outclassed."

"Is that all, Quinton?"

"Mr. President — Laurie —" Quinton pleaded now. "Look, you just can't *do* it. Anyhow, military law prohibits duelling, you know that. We— we'll have to stop you!"

There was noise again.

"Be *quiet!*" There was a lash of discipline in Giroux's voice. "You *cannot* stop me. My message of acceptance went an hour ago. It is already being broadcast to the world. General Quinton, I am as expert in the weapon I have chosen as Marshal Feng can be. My physical condition is more than adequate to its employment. As for legality, we'll fight in Uruguay, where duelling's legal. Besides—" He stopped; regarded them. "What the hell do you propose to do about it? Use violence? Mount a quick palace revolution? Don't be damned fools. I am not only President of the United States, gentlemen. I am

Commander-in-Chief of our armed forces. I have already issued orders to those immediately concerned."

State pushed his chair back. Blood draining from his face, he stood erect. "I cannot be a party to this— this savagery, th-this absurdity. Man, can't you think what you'll be doing to this country's image everywhere? To your own? I— I *resign*."

"Earneshaw," Giroux said, "what will Feng do to our image if I ignore him? If I refuse to fight? Don't you see— it may be I won't win, but I can't *lose*. Even if he kills me, Feng can't win. And if any of you does try to stop me — if you so much as *try* — what will that do to our country's image when the news gets out? What will it do for Feng?"

He sat down slowly and deliberately. The others hesitated, weighing the chances, each trying to guess what all the rest would do. Almost imperceptibly, the Joint Chiefs seemed to move in a little closer to each other, to the President.

Quinton seated himself immediately. Finally, muttering, the Secretary of State lowered himself into his chair. Their breathing was the only sound.

"For a long time," said the President, "something has been needed to clear the air. To clear it of Feng, preferably. I'll grant you my acceptance is a break with all tradition, with diplomatic usage, but — believe me — I know what I am doing."

"That's asking us to take a lot on faith," Quinton put in. "I'll grant you, sir, you've called your shots right in the past, but—"

"Feng and I will fight at three o'clock tomorrow afternoon. With weapons of my own choosing, under conditions set by me. Exactly equal weapons and conditions, naturally. No practice will be necessary for either of us. And each of us will bring three seconds, including an interpreter."

"Who will they be, sir?" Navy asked.

Giroux smiled. "First, if he cares to come, Lieutenant-General Quinton, who has watched me shoot. Major Harrison Ouyang, of Air-Space, who will interpret for our side. And Sergeant Easting, Sergeant-Major of the Army, who holds the Congressional from Vietnam and who was good enough to carry my message to the Chinese Embassy," Giroux saw annoyance on the face of Navy. "I myself will represent our service, Admiral," he explained. "Who Feng's seconds will turn out to be, I, of course, do not know. That is all, gentlemen. Turn on your televisions tomorrow. Our encounter will probably get worldwide coverage, live."

"Or dead," the Secretary of State said through his teeth.

"Or dead," the President agreed. He rose, making a gesture of dismissal. They filed out, bearing a strange silence, and politely he walked them to the door.

Quinton, last to leave, held back a little. "How'd I do?" he whispered.

"Beautifully, Tom, beautifully." The President touched his shoulder. "Just like you'd never heard a word about it."

"You're *still* nuts," Quinton growled.

The world press reacted — unpredictably, chaotically, often hysterically. Frequently, policy was drowned under the enthusiasm of newsmen — enthusiasm for unsuspected courage, for the brave cutting of a Gordian knot, for lost chivalry, for Giroux himself. Only very rarely was there enthusiasm for Feng, and that, as *Le Monde* later pointed out, was usually of an "or else" variety. There were solemn and prestigious protests in the United Nations — protests which went round and round and ended nowhere. The temperate Scandinavians, the Dutch, the Indians, the more leftish Britons disapproved — but their disapproval was usually of the principle, and seldom of the man. The French, not too surprisingly, changed sides at once, recalled the duels of men like Clemenceau, attributed Giroux's most admirable sense of personal and national honor to his Gallic ancestry.

The press at home was even more confusing and confused. The San Francisco *Chronicle-Examiner* perhaps outdid the rest. It ran three major editorials: one damned President Giroux as a racist Southerner bent on national suicide; another compared him quite favorably with Generals Andrew Jackson and MacArthur; the third said flatly that no institution as evil as the duel could possibly solve problems which were sociologically insoluble.

Secretary of State Earneshaw resigned, as publicly as possible, and demanded instant emergency action by the Congress. Neither the Congress nor the press paid much attention to him. Before the subject could even be brought up in either House, Giroux was on his way — and every politician knew that, in spite of any odds, he *might* come back the winner. It was no time for self-commitment, nor for drastic action.

Before he went to bed that night, the President said his good-byes to his lady. He told her that he loved her, and they remembered something 30 years gone by, something small, and really unimportant, and very precious only to themselves. She knew already what he planned to do.

Paper Tiger

He kissed her, and she asked, "How—how are you going to fight him, Loring?"

He looked away from her. "Like Cousin Kerby fought the steamboat man."

"I was afraid of that," she whispered, remembering all the details of that duel a century and a quarter in the past, when Kerby Loring and the steamboat man had met each other on the Mississippi. *"I was afraid of that."*

Then, to make things easier, the President said, very softly, "Good-bye, Jen," and kissed her through her tears, and went away.

Next day, when his plane set down at Montevideo Airport, he seemed fresh and rested, though some observers thought they saw signs of strain around his mouth. He met a hero's welcome. The President of Uruguay was an old fishing and poker playing friend, from OAS days; before either of them had been a President, they had exchanged visits in each other's houses, in each other's countries. Besides, Fernando Estrada Orde had himself fought a duel or two, with sabres, once against another Uruguayan colonel, again with a combative professor-journalist. Now, under his properly sober brows, his eyes were flashing, for the personal drama which his friend was facing, for the unprecedented history which would soon be made. They walked together to the waiting limousines, under the guns of four protecting armored cars.

"Feng is here," Estrada said, when they were under way. "He arrived less than an hour ago. I have given him an unusually heavy escort." He smiled, showing his strong teeth. "I almost hope he violates our hospitality. I do not like the man."

"All the arrangements have been made?" Giroux asked, in Spanish.

"*Sí*. My military aide went out this morning, with the North Korean minister and some sort of delegate from Beijing, and they bought the ammunition and the guns. My aide did not choose the shops; they did. They bought four guns, as you requested — in four separate places. They are being very careful."

"*Naturalmente*. And the rest?"

"As you specified. Feng has been shown your requirements. He has agreed to meet you in an empty office in our Ministry of Agriculture, where there is room for TV cameras. From there, you and he will go into the other room, where all is as you wanted it, but that room he does not know about."

"Otherwise he is satisfied?"

"*De seguro*. He says that he can kill you anywhere."

There was a silence, before Estrada asked, "How do you propose to fight this man, my friend? Now we have bought the tools, how will you use them?"

He listened to the explanation. Then he spoke very softly: "I should not say this thing to you, *amigo*. I should never say it to the head of a great and friendly state. But do you realize that you are mad?"

"How would *you* fight him?"

"I have watched him. I would never fight him unless I absolutely had to."

"I have to," said the President of the United States.

They entered the small room simultaneously, by adjoining doors, each group escorted by four Uruguayan officers. The room was new and bare, its slate-gray walls forbidding. Between the doors a table stood, guarded by two more Uruguayans and a grim Chinese. On it there were four double-barreled shotguns, a box of shells.

Feng was in his marshal's uniform. In the flesh, he seemed even taller, harder, straighter than on the screen. His cold eyes had taken in the room; obviously he did not like what he had seen. He was speaking to one of his three seconds who, like Quinton and Ouyang and Sergeant Easting, were armed with submachine guns. They were burly men, obviously military but with more than a hint of secret police about them. Loring Giroux was the only man there out of uniform; he wore slacks and a good tweed jacket.

"Sir, he's been asking whether he's on TV," Major Ouyang said, *sotto voce*. "They've told him that he is, and he's annoyed because there's just one camera. It looks like he's going to make a speech."

Almost immediately, lights went on dazzlingly, and the familiar tirade started.

"Want me to translate it, sir? It's the same malarkey, only he's accusing you of trickery, with compliments. He says he's going to kill you anyhow."

"Don't bother," Loring Giroux answered. "I've heard it all before." He watched Feng's mobile face, and listened to the ranting voice, and wondered whether he had underestimated him, or overestimated him, or— Abruptly, his mind flashed him a picture of Ouyang, of his expression when he had looked at Feng. Ouyang's own parents, he recalled, had been in China when the Reds took over.

"Major—" He smiled at him. "—let's try and keep it cool, shall we?"

As suddenly as it had started, the speech was over, and Feng was barking questions.

"Sir, he wants to know what the picture is."

"Tell him," the President replied, speaking very clearly, "that we are going to fight with two of those four shotguns. Tell him that they were chosen by his own people, not by ours, and that there was no time for pre-arrangement or collusion. Tell him to pick two guns, then to select one of them for himself. I will take one of the two remaining."

They waited while the Marshal and his seconds made a choice. Then Giroux made his. He picked a double-trigger brush gun, with 25-inch barrels, by Francotte, opened it, checked safety, locks, and firing-pins.

"Now, Mr. President, this Feng demands to know where you will fight."

"Say that I will tell him after we enter the next room. We will go first."

They then went through the door, which an Uruguayan brigadier opened for them; and, carefully and suspiciously, Feng and his seconds followed them. It was a room slightly larger than the other, windowless, equally slate gray. It was glaringly illuminated for the TV cameras which, raised on platforms high above the floor, stared down through armor plate. Dead center, there was a standard poker table, with two chairs. There was an armor screen, placed so the seconds, three on either side, would hold the table in their field of fire — but not each other.

"What does this mean?" Feng demanded.

"Tell him," Giroux said, "It means that we will fight here, in this room. Tell him that in my part of the United States, many years ago, we had a type of duel which men fought only when nothing else could settle a dispute — when neither would be satisfied with less. We will sit together at that poker table, he and I. Face to face, we will aim our loaded shotguns at each other, our fingers on the triggers. Then we will wait while the countdown clock—" he pointed at the wall — "ticks off one minute. The last ten seconds will be counted out loud. When it comes round to zero, we will fire — together. If either of us fires prematurely, the other's seconds will be free to kill him. It is all very simple."

Feng listened to his interpreter's translation, and as he listened his brows drew down like gathering thunderclouds. His voice erupted in a burst of rage.

Loring Giroux waited for no translation. "Ask him," he said. "Is he afraid?"

Ouyang snapped out a few contemptuous words of Mandarin. There was no answer. Momentarily, a look of calculation flickered across the anger on Feng's face. Then, spitting on the floor viciously, he strode towards the table.

Briefly, after that, politeness and formality took over. Two Uruguayan field officers stood behind each chair. They bowed to the two duellists. They seated them. They ushered the two groups of seconds into position, the Americans with their Smith & Wesson 9mm caseless submachine guns on one side of the impenetrable screen, the Chinese with their approximately equal pieces on the other. Then the Uruguayans left the room, closing the door behind them.

The brigadier stepped forward. "Gentlemen," he asked, "are you ready?"

Loring Giroux, looking into the twin muzzles of Feng's gun, said, "I am ready."

Feng nodded silently.

The brigadier stepped back out of the seconds' field of fire. "*Begin!*" he ordered.

The countdown clock began to tick. Like every fatal, final clock, it ticked with an immense and deadly slowness.

Sixty.

And *fifty-nine.*

And *fifty-eight...*

While the world held its breath, Loring Giroux raised his eyes to the unfamiliar and unfathomable eyes confronting him. He had done this at many another poker table, not always at completely friendly games. But it had not been like this. He felt the mounting tension in the room, the silent-screaming tautness of friends and enemies...

And *fifty-seven.*

And *fifty-six.*

And—

Strangely, his own tenseness did not mount. He knew he was afraid, but it was as though he rode his fear with tightly gathered reins. Looking into those eyes, into their blacknesses, he thought, *Did I read him right? Have I succeeded in reading him at all? What sort of hand does he think he's holding? What does he make of me? Now that he knows what this is all about, how is he really taking it? He must've thought he had it figured out just now when he decided to shut up and fight...* The chances were, he thought, that Feng had then remembered his own much younger, better trained reactions. Well...

The clock ticked on, but Loring Giroux made no attempt to keep account of it. Forty seconds were left to go, perhaps. Forty, or thirty-eight, or thirty-nine. It made no difference, that time to certain death. *Here!* He brought

Paper Tiger

himself up short. *Now that's no way to think.* He saw the cable-tightness of Feng's jaw, and wondered whether Feng too felt fear. *This is how the world stands today*, he thought. *Like this Chinese and me. That is why he and I must kill each other—*

Suddenly his fear welled up within him, and the certain outcome, whose certainty he had not fully dared to face, confronted him, and through his mind flowed all those thoughts which come to men who know that they must die. Thoughts of those loved, those lost, those who would never touch his hand again. He tried to tell himself that even though he died his country could not lose. Nor could the world. Feng could not win.

Oh, God! Were there now only twenty seconds between him and death? Twenty? Or twenty-five? Perhaps fifteen?

He dropped his eyes. He saw the fingers of Marshal Feng's left hand, around the fore end of the pointed gun. Five precious seconds passed before he comprehended their significance. Their knuckles were beginning to run white, and on the index finger's tip stood one small drop of sweat. And there was one thing more.

Then his own fear fell away, and he raised his eyes again, and looked once more into the eyes of Feng Teh-chih, and smiled.

"*Ten!*" called the Uruguayan brigadier.

Slowly, with the ticking clock, he counted down, while the Marshal and the President measured the death that lay between them. The brigadier's own voice rising high against his will, he counted down to *Six*, to *Five*, to *Four*...

And, with four seconds left, Feng very deliberately put his shotgun on the table, and stood up.

It was an excellent performance. His face, carefully composed, showed only anger and contempt. Even his voice, at first, was thoroughly controlled. "This is an idiocy!" he said. "Did you think that I, Feng Teh-chih, would really sit and play your stupid game?" Then suddenly he yelled, "It can prove nothing, nothing, *nothing!* I shall not let the Chinese people be cheated by this trick of the imperialists! *Never!* I— I shall yet defeat you, weak Giroux!"

Loring Giroux, of course, did not learn what he had said until he heard it translated later— but he divined its meaning. "Well, Marshal Feng," he answered, "are you leaving us? These shotguns are as nothing compared to H-bombs. Surely you aren't going to give up so good a chance to prove that I'm a paper tiger?"

Feng did not wait for a translation. He sent his chair crashing to the floor. He bellowed to his seconds. Without another word, he marched out through the door, and they followed him.

Loring Giroux knew that death left with them. Gradually his fingers on the shotgun relaxed. Mechanically, he opened the gun, took out the shells. He pushed his own chair back—

Then there was tumult all around him. Estrada Orde had pulled him to his feet and was embracing him. Major Ouyang was doing his best to shake his hand. Quinton, swearing mightily, was pounding him on the back. Newsmen were swarming in, and the TV crews were practically hysterical. Champagne, as if by magic, had appeared out of nowhere.

It was not until some hours afterwards, when finally they were relaxing in the plane, that General Quinton said, "My God, that was tight there for a while.

Paper Tiger

Laurie, I would've sworn that guy would never chicken out."

"He didn't," the President replied.

"*Sir?*"

"He didn't. He's no coward. He's just completely practical; he'd never give his life unless he'd win by doing it — undying fame, perhaps. At least a victory. He had me buffaloed for just a minute though — until I saw his hands. He wasn't keyed up half enough— not for a man who'd put on all those raving acts. His hands were tight, but they weren't tight enough, and they were steady as a rock. It was then I knew he wouldn't go the route, that he was waiting for *me* to back down. He's not a poker player."

"What about that threat that he'd defeat you later?"

"That was for the home folks. Now he's going to try and play another hand. He figures he'll get it all explained away, or if not, he'll simply polish off the opposition. That was the reason for hinting that he'd planned it. This time, I think he's wrong. I think he's done for. His people don't like losers."

A fortnight later, Loring Giroux dismissed a special evening meeting of his Cabinet, and went upstairs to where his wife was waiting. He scratched the sheepdog by the desk. He rubbed Beauregard's smug whiskers. "That cat's getting fatter than a pig," he said. "What you been feeding him?"

She smiled at him. "Shrimp, liver, and filet mignon."

"He has it coming. He's no paper tiger." He returned her smile. "You've heard the news?"

"Feng?"

"Yes, he's down the drain. But, Jen, that isn't all. The Chinese have just sent a message to the world. They want no cross-the-table shotgun duels; they said exactly that. They want to settle all outstanding differences. It's just been broadcast."

She came to him, and took his hands, and kissed him on the lips. "Oh, God!" she whispered. "Like Cousin Kerby fought the steamboat man— Oh, *thank God!*"

Then Loring Giroux put his arm around her, and led her to the doors that gave out on the balcony, and threw them open.

They stood there together, breathing the clear new air.

14
Fungo the Unrighteous

"Fungo the Unrighteous" was first published in Amazing Stories 61, *in November, 1986. This is the story's first inclusion in an anthology.*

It was the great good fortune of the people of the Triple Kingdom of Upper, Middle, and Lower Vuthland that they never experienced the political uncertainty besetting their neighbors, for from the day their sovereign ascended the throne to the day of his (or her) death, the course of the reign was as fixed and determined as the procession of the suns. It was a splendidly simple system. When it came time for the incumbent to die in battle, or (far more commonly) to perish of a surfeit of lampreys, or to be sleeping slain (as was of course right and proper), the royal astrologer would convene the entire membership of the three Royal Vuthlandian Colleges of Astrologers, Diviners, and Soothsayers, and they would solemnly attend a beasting, where they would consult the entrails of a virgin male cwisamp (of the footed variety). Then they would proclaim the name the heir to the throne would bear, the character he would assume, the number of years he would reign, and the date and manner of his death.

It worked wonderfully. For centuries, the kingdom had been ruled by such memorable figures as Grundius the Ungodly (802-847), Throd Tanglewit (870-879),

The Timeless Tales of Reginald Bretnor

Hargust the Torturer (1055-1102), Scrandeg the Conqueror (1147-1152), the infamous Waltzing Matilda (1205-1233, about whom a song was written hundreds of years later), Aproprong the Profligate (1256-1286), and Herf the Merciful (August 1314).

Now it so happened that in the fall of 1388, when Yarskald Throatbiter was all set to die in the third year of his reign, next in line for the crown was a handsome young prince named Fungo. He had every virtue. He was always merry and openhanded, kindly and courteous. He loved to go off for days, dancing and singing with the Gypsies, with whom he was a great favorite. (Their queen, an ancient crone called Mama Gabor, had formally adopted him into her tribe.) He was a great horseman, and a great hunter and swordsman as well. Indeed, if he can be said to have had any fault whatsoever, it was in his extreme naiveté. This deeply distressed the lovely Lady Clysomel, with whom he was madly in love and who loved him dearly, for she was the stepniece of Kostra Karbunkel, the royal astrologer now for more than one reign — a bitter, lecherous, treacherous old man who was also, by a royal edict he had connived for, her legal guardian.

So, when it became known that Yarskald was on his deathbed, she pleaded with Fungo to take her away, to flee far from the three Vuthlands. "Let's take swift horses, my love," she begged. "There are those in your stables none other can catch. We'll take gold and jewels enough, and our most faithful servants. Even if we cannot be king and queen, we shall be happy." And she began to weep softly.

Gently, Fungo smoothed her glistening black tresses, and gently he tried to dissuade her. "Beautiful

Fungo the Unrighteous

Clysomel, you shall indeed be a queen. Before the week's out, you shall be *my* queen. I cannot believe that your step-uncle, unpleasant as he undoubtedly is, can wish anyone as sweet and charming as you any real harm."

"Harm?" she cried, "Fungo, he not only wishes me *harm* — he wants *me*, that vile old man! He wants me for *himself*. And the Gods only know what he'll read in that poor cwisamp's entrails at the beasting."

But Fungo was much too innocent to believe her, for it was not in him to think that anyone could be as cruel and as despicable as she had painted her uncle. So, when the old man had departed, she betook herself, escorted only by one trusted groom, to the camp of the Gypsies in a birch forest near Farvath, the capital city, and there she bared her heart to old Mama Gabor.

Gravely, shaking her head once in a while, the ancient Gypsy listened to her. She read the lines in her right hand and the lines in her left. For perhaps fifteen minutes, she peered intently into a crystal ball that gleamed on the table between them. She consulted a curious and frightening tarot deck known only to the Gypsies of Vuthland. Finally, she clapped her wrinkled hands, and a pretty young Gypsy came in with a smoking samovar on a tray, and teacups, and Mama Gabor showed the Lady Clysomel how to swirl the leaves around after she'd finished her third cup.

Then, staring at the pattern of the leaves, she spoke. "Soon, soon," she said, "you, dear child, you and your good Prince will suffer distress which you will think you cannot survive. The old man whom you fear will part you. He is determined on a terrible destiny for Prince Fungo, and one even more terrible for you. What he is even now reading in the entrails is what his own twisted mind dictates, and he will proclaim it tomorrow at the enthronement. ... Hush, hush, my dear!" She soothed as Clysomel burst into tears. "Though you are facing something unspeakable, you must not lose heart. No, no! You must hasten back to the Palace with this message from Mama Gabor for Prince Fungo. Listen well! Tell him I say that when he is ordered to do evil, as he will be, he must *not* follow his true nature and refuse. Instead, he must wait till we Gypsies come up to kneel at the throne, for that is when he must ask me one question, which I have written on this piece of paper. Tell him, and tell him again, my Lady — for all will then depend upon him. But he must not unfold the paper until that very moment!"

So the Lady Clysomel, somewhat heartened, hastened back to the Palace, sought out the Prince, and told him all that had occurred. He, of course, took little notice of it, but simply to set her mind at ease he took Mama Gabor's message and promised faithfully that he would ask the question written in it when the time came.

Yarskald Throatbiter died at seven of the evening, exactly on schedule, and at once bells began tolling and trumpets and conchs started braying all through the land, informing the folk that the king was duly dead and they would have a new king on the morrow.

Naturally, they had already assembled by tens of thousands: rough, surly Lower Vuthlanders in their hairy goatskin breeks; sleek Mid-Vuthian silk and spice merchants and subtle artisans; gangling, boastful mountaineers from Upper Vuthland all swaggering in cwisamphide capes and bragging in coarse nasal voices. Everyone who could possibly get away was there, for the en-

Fungo the Unrighteous

thronement of the new king was the most exciting event of many a year, and till it was accomplished no plans could be made, no courses of action decided upon either in business or agriculture or even in matters of romance. But the crowds were in excellent spirits, for they all knew that Fungo was heir to the throne, and all wished him well.

Immediately after the death of the king, Prince Fungo was ceremonially taken in charge by, among others, the Lord Chamberlain, and solemnly invested with the regalia and raiment of Majesty: the Great Necklace heavy with beautifully polished cwisamp gizzard-stones, the mace, the sword of power (which had, incidentally, been used to end four previous reigns), the three crowns symbolizing each of the realms, and the enormously heavy robes of the sovereign.

Encumbered with these, Fungo presided at the ritual banquet, at which any number of dignitaries devoured the late king's funereal meats. He would much rather have been with his Clysomel, but he did what he knew was his duty, telling himself that next day, right after his enthronement, he and she would be united in marriage.

He slept well that night, breakfasted cheerfully, and shortly afterwards suffered himself to be escorted to the great square facing the palace, where it seems the entire population of the country had assembled, cheering themselves hoarse. The throne stood on a dais which had three levels, surrounded by a squadron of Royal Guard cavalry and a battalion of Royal Guard infantry. On its lowest level stood the Lord Mayor of Farvuth, many members of the petty nobility, and the more worshipful sort of civil servants. On the next level up, the great nobles were proudly arrayed, all in their picturesque regional costume and gaudy with decorations and gems. But on the highest level of all, besides the generals of the Royal Guard (of whom there were several), there was only Kostra Karbunkel and a score of his most important fellow astrologers, diviners, and soothsayers.

Fungo ascended the steps to the throne, pausing occasionally to acknowledge a bow or a curtsey, or allow his hand to be kissed, but doing so very abstractedly, for his mind was on Clysomel, who was nowhere in sight.

"Pray seat yourself, Majesty," said the royal astrologer, his voice like a crow's caw, and his dry, narrow face a mask of unconcealed triumph. Fungo, looking at him, saw that on an ivory table at his side was a silver salver bearing the cwisamp entrails that had decided his fate. They smelled dreadful, and he wrinkled his nose. "Where is Clysomel?" he demanded.

Karbunkel leered. "She's been told to stay home, Sire, for she has no part in these ceremonies — no, nor in your royal future." His thin tongue darted out, licked his lips. "But I have other nice little plans for her, never fear!"

We'll see about that! Fungo thought grimly, but he forced himself to say nothing.

Then Karbunkel blew a single shrill note on an ancient horn he drew from his robes. "Let the rites proceed!" he proclaimed; and he was instantly echoed by eighty stentorial heralds stationed in every part of the square.

First the generals of the Guard came up, knelt before Fungo, and swore absolute obedience to his every word and whim. Then the greater nobility did likewise,

Fungo the Unrighteous

followed by the lesser nobles, the Lord Mayor, and the civil servants.

There was a moment of breathless silence while Karbunkel stood there, both arms held up to heaven. "And now," he declared, "*Now you shall learn what the history of our King Fungo's reign shall be, as revealed by these infallible significators!*" And he pointed at the entrails, over which a great many flies were now buzzing.

"*You, Noble King, from this moment on shall be known to all men as* FUNGO THE UNRIGHTEOUS! *You shall exact the cruelest taxes in our long history! You shall ravish maidens, and have innocent men put to death! Your name will be a stench in the nostrils, and will be reviled throughout the length and breadth of the Three Kingdoms! You will savagely persecute all those of whom the royal astrologers disapprove, especially the Gypsies! You shall be cursed by rich and poor alike, for your every act from this moment on — from this most auspicious moment on — shall damn you as enemy of all righteous men and all righteousness! You shall marry the Princess Savaka of Utt, and with her you will sleep every night of your life—*"

Here a great groan rose from the crowd, for not only were they all deeply shocked at the prognostication, but they knew that the Princess Savaka was renowned for her promiscuity and foul temper.

"*—and—*" cried out Clysomel's step-uncle, raising his voice, "*you shall rule for the term of 12 years, 9 months, and 8 days, and shall perish finally of fish-spears thrust severally through you! I have spoken!*"

Fungo was thoroughly stricken. He sat on his throne, trying manfully to hold back his tears and to keep his hands from trembling too visibly, and conscious that he was pale as a ghost. He had almost cried out that the last thing he wanted was to be the *Unrighteous*, but fortunately he had remembered the message. The astrologer bowed to him mockingly, then stepped aside so that the traditional approach of the King's subjects to the foot of the throne could begin.

Usually, at this point in the ceremony, there was a mighty shouting from the multitude, a blaring of horns and a ruffle of drums, an eager pealing of bells, as people surged forward to pledge their loyalty. Now there was a dead silence. No one moved.

Then suddenly, out of the crowd, the new king beheld two figures approaching. The first, wearing bright silken robes and garlands of precious gold coins, was Mama Gabor, tall and erect in spite of her age. Her companion, obviously younger, was similarly garbed but had her face veiled demurely.

"*Let the old witch approach, Majesty,*" hissed Kostra Karbunkel in King Fungo's ear, "*then tell her what persecutions you have in mind for her, ha-ha-ha!*"

Fungo had been fumbling nervously in his purse, fearful that he might have misplaced the message, but finally he'd found it. Now, surreptitiously, he unfolded and read it.

"Your Majesty," he read, "you must ask me this question: *Mother Gabor, must I obey the cruel prophesy about my behavior, which is so much against my real nature?* Then you must not be surprised at my answer. Fear not."

As Mama Gabor knelt at his feet, he reached his hand out to her. In a loud, strong, clear voice, he asked her the question, and throughout the square the eighty heralds repeated it.

"Lord," answered the Gypsy. "No man has ever dared to dispute the auguries, so you must obey. You

Fungo the Unrighteous

must obey literally and without reservation. You must become the enemy of all righteous men, and the more righteous they are, the more cruel must you be to them." Her black eyes glittered, and she winked at him. Then she stared directly at Kostra Karbunkel. "The most righteous first!"

King Fungo, naive though he was, was by no means stupid. He stood. He looked at Clysomel's step-uncle. "Mother Gabor," he said to the Gypsy, "you can read the future, and you can delve into the natures of men. Who is the most righteous man in my kingdom?"

"Who but your esteemed royal astrologer?" replied Mama Gabor.

King Fungo thereupon drew the glistening sword of power. "She speaks truth!" he declared. "I, Fungo the Unrighteous, shall commence my reign with the most unrighteous deed anyone can imagine. Ho! To me, generals of the Guard!"

They came to him at the double.

"Seize that man!" he ordered, pointing at Kostra. "Bind him hand and foot. Throw him into a dung-cart, and take him forthwith to the stinking bogs and fens of our Lower Vuthland. There let him be thrown to the cwisamps (those of the footless variety) who now are in rut!"

Kostra Karbunkel struggled to prostrate himself at the King's feet, but the generals restrained him. "Merciful Lord!" he shrieked. "How can you do so evil a deed? Don't you know that footless cwisamps in rut are so mad and mindless that they have no idea of species at all? Think what will become of me!"

"I *am*," King Fungo replied levelly, and the generals bound the weeping man hand and foot and bore him away. "And I think all my loyal subjects, gathered here together, will agree that it's about as beautifully unrighteous as anything you could imagine. And now, Mother Gabor, who is the *second* most righteous man in the kingdom?"

She did not answer, but both she and the King turned to look at the first assistant royal astrologer, a very fat man named Whelpstone.

The King nodded. "Yes, I think so," he said with a very cold smile. "Yes, *indeed*."

At that, poor Whelpstone came forward, quivering and shaking. "Majestic King!" he exclaimed. "I— I— we— that is— we've been considering those entrails. Yes, we have. We have reached a conclusion. Kostra Karbunkel misread those entrails. Oh yes, completely. His prognostication was full of gross errors. May we have your royal permission to examine them one more time?"

"*If you hurry!*" King Fungo replied. "You may consider them while the crowd sings our royal anthem. After that, I want them thrown away. Those flies are unbearable."

It was later remarked that never had the 28 verses of the anthem been sung so enthusiastically, and when the last mighty chords had died away, the whole square seemed to be waiting.

"*Well?*" King Fungo said to Whelpstone.

"Your Heroic Majesty, yes, yes, we have reexamined the entrails— and they've been thrown away, as you ordered, though I must say they were as fine a set of entrails as ever I've seen. I *can't* understand how Karbunkel, poor old man, went so far wrong with them. They were clear as crystal, Noble Sire—"

"Come to the point," ordered the King.

Fungo the Unrighteous

"Ha-ha! I shall, I shall. The point is that, first and foremost, it should *not* have been *Un*righteous. No, never. The entrails were explicit. Sir, you should have been Fungo the *Up*righteous, a horse of a very different color—"

"*Very*," the King agreed.

"And he wasn't only wrong about that, no indeed! He also was wrong about what you would do, for it was indisputable that under your benign, wise rule crops will improve, there'll be no crime to speak of, we'll have excellent foreign relations and a most favorable balance of trade, and you'll lower taxes dramatically. And not only that, my Lord, not only *that* — he was also wrong about the length of your reign, which will last 55 years 11 months, and at least 19 days, after which you and your Queen will succumb very peacefully of old age—"

"My *Queen*?" said King Fungo, with an edge to his voice.

"Oh, yes, Majesty, he was wrong about that, too. You aren't going to marry Princess Savaka. I can't imagine how he could've missed it— you're going to marry Lady Clysomel, his very own step-niece, and you're going to marry her this very day, right after supper!"

At that point, Mama Gabor's companion dropped her veil, and King Fungo saw that she was indeed Clysomel. Instantly, he stepped down from the throne, put his arm around her, and brought her to sit there beside him. (It was a very wide throne.)

Of course, the heralds had dutifully echoed everything that was said, and now the assembled Vuthlanders became almost hysterical, shouting "LONG LIVE GOOD KING FUNGO! LONG LIVE FUNGO THE *UP*RIGHTEOUS!" and singing verses of the royal anthem.

In the midst of it, Whelpstone approached the royal couple. "Would Your Majesties, er, that is— would you consider me staying on as — as astrologer general?" he asked timidly.

"As long as you mind your Ps and Qs," answered good King Fungo.

That night there was revelry in all three Vuthlands, singing and carousing and good humor and dancing in the streets.

King Fungo and Queen Clysomel had been duly married and put to bed, destined to reign for at least 55 years, 11 months, and 19 days, to have several beautiful and intelligent children, and to leave behind them a country happier and more prosperous than it ever had been.

And as to what befell Kostra Karbunkel in the stinking bogs and fens of Lower Vuthland, the less said the better.

15
All the Tea in China

"All the Tea in China," which was first published in The Magazine of Fantasy & Science Fiction 20 *in May, 1961, was included in* The 7th Annual of the Year's Best SF, *edited by Judith Merril, in 1962. This book was first published in hardcover by Simon & Schuster in New York, then as a paperback by Dell Publishing, New York, and by Tokyo Sogen-sha Company in Japan, and, as* The Best of Sci-Fi — Two, *by Mayflower-Dell in London.*

It was mighty lucky for me that my Grandma Whitford caught on in time. If she hadn't, chances are I would've grown up just like her Great-uncle Jonas Hackett, and come to the same sort of end, shaking hands with the Devil himself before breakfast, and with not even a Christian tombstone over me at the last for folks to come look at.

I was down in an empty stall in the barn, making a trade with Jim Bledsoe. Jim was snivelling and crying and begging me not to make him go through with the trade, and I wasn't giving an inch.

He picked up his 12-gauge Iver-Johnson, and his two Belgian hares, and his skates, and fondled them kind of, and put them back down with the rest of his stuff; and he said, maybe for the twentieth time, "Aw, B-Bill, you—you can have all the rest. But p-p-please lemme keep my old shotgun, *p-please.*"

And I said, "Not for all the tea in China, I won't. No sirree bob!"

It was right then Grandma showed up, her little eyes crackling and sparkling, and her lips set as tight as when she was mad at some fresh city peddler. Small as she was, she grabbed my left ear and twisted real hard.

"Ow!" I said.

She twisted again. "All the tea in China, indeed!" she snapped. "I'll all-the-tea-in-China you, boy. Now you give those things back to Jimmy—this instant! And Jimmy, you take 'em and skeddaddle on home."

"Aw, Gran'ma," I grumbled, "we're only making a *trade*. There's nothing wrong with just—*Yow!*"

"Don't lie to me, boy. You were chiseling him out of his eyeteeth. That whole big pile for a one-bladed jackknife and a busted war sword! It's that bad Hackett blood in you, I do declare. You're getting to be as wicked and sinful as Great-uncle Jonas."

She looked at Jimmy again, who was fiddling around, still scared to pick up his things. "Go ahead, take 'em," she told him. "The sheriff won't ever hear how you burned down his outhouse—that's a promise. When I get through with Bill here, he won't say a word." She twisted my ear harder than ever. "No sirree bob—not for all the tea in China, he won't!"

And as soon as Jimmy had beat it, she marched me out of the barn, and straight past the house while the hired-hand snickered, and around the big corn-patch and right up the east slope of Hackett's Hill. She didn't slow down or let go of my ear till we got clean to the top; and even though Hackett's Hill isn't more than a couple hundred feet high, I was just about out of breath.

She told me to sit. "Wonder why I brought you here?"

All the Tea in China

Hackett's Hill wasn't worth climbing. It was sort of lumpy and brown, with nothing but scrubby dry weeds growing on it. All you could see from the top was the Post Road winding around it before straightening out down the valley, and our house, and Smathers'. So I nodded.

"I brought you," she said, "because it was right about here that Jonas Hackett's place was before he was took by the Devil, and because I can see his spirit's strong in you, and because I aim to drive it clean out."

She stared at me till it seemed that a cold little wind blew across Hackett's Hill and into my spine. "Boy," she asked, "what do you want to be when you' grown?"

I looked down at my shoes. "I want to be rich," I told her defiantly. "I want to move down to Boston, and have a big house, and a carriage, and a gold watch and chain, and tell folks what to do."

"I *thought* so," she said. "Well, that's all right for some, whose natures are honest and can stand off temptation—but it isn't for you. You're going to Harvard College instead, and let 'em make you a doctor."

"No, *ma'am*," I answered right back. "I wouldn't do that. No, siree bob. Not for—" Then I remembered my ear and shut up.

"*Not for all the tea in China*," she finished up for me. "*No siree bob*. And that's just what Great-uncle Jonas answered them back when they wanted *him* to go down to Harvard. Now you sit real still, and don't interrupt, and I'll tell you the story. Only don't go telling anyone else, because it's nothing we're proud of, and it's best kept in the family."

She gave me a look, and I promised....

The Timeless Tales of Reginald Bretnor

By the time Jonas was 40 (Grandma said), he was a fine-looking man. Maybe he was a little too lean, and I guess his eyes looked a little too much like cold chunks of gray glass in dark caves. They say, too, that his big, pale hands were always opening and closing all by themselves, as if they were hungry. But he had curly black hair, and a good set of white teeth, and a walk like a lion out hunting.

(In my mind, I saw Great-uncle Jonas clear as could be, and I shivered.)

Besides (she went on), by that time he owned a good part of the land around here, and had loans out on lots more. He had some business in Boston, and down in New York, which he kept to himself. But everyone knew that he owned a three-quarter share in the tea-clipper *Queen of the East*, because everyone knew young Middleton Martin, who was her first mate and the one friend Jonas had in the world.

You'd have thought there'd have been lots of men willing to call him their friend, and plenty of women hereabouts to marry him at the drop of a hat. But there weren't. Only Middleton Martin forgave him for the things he had done—maybe because he'd been off to sea so much of the time, and never seen Jonas at work. You see, boy, Jonas was never content just making a dollar. He had to make it *off* someone, so it hurt—and the more it hurt the better he liked it.

Let's say a neighbor had something that'd just about kill him if anyone knew, and Jonas found out. Pretty soon he'd show up and offer to buy the man's team, or his pasture, or even his house. He'd look it over, taking his time, and they'd have a talk, friendly like, and finally they'd get to the price—and Jonas'd offer a dollar, or maybe fifteen, or fifty at the outside. Usually his neighbor would shout he was crazy. Then Jonas would tighten the screws. He'd whisper what he'd found out. He'd let the man cuss and threaten, and argue and beg. He'd pretend to give in. And right at the last, he'd tighten his jaw and say, "No siree bob. Not for all the tea in China, I won't."

(Grandma paused for a minute, but I just pulled at the dry grass at my feet instead of looking up at her.)

He always did it that way (Grandma said). It was the same when he'd clamp down on a loan. He was hated by every man, woman, and child within fifteen miles. He'd built a fine, big, new house, and he lived there alone except for two foreign servants he'd brought in from the city. He never went out to visit, even his kin, or showed up at church, or had anyone over except Middleton Martin. And all through the years, he never so much as looked at one of the girls. Then all of a sudden, when he'd turned 40, he started courting Mary Ann Thorpe.

She was the prettiest girl in the valley, 20 years younger than he, with hair like honey. It was known that Jonas had a money hold on her father, but what really started tongues wagging was that she'd been promised to Middleton Martin for close on three years. A few said it was queer that Jonas Hackett would do such a thing to the one friend he had, but mostly folks thought it was just like his nature. She was Middleton's girl, and no man could find anyone finer; and betraying a friendship just made him want her the more. The whole valley waited for the *Queen of the East* to come back with her cargo of tea. And because Jonas was Middleton's friend, and for fear of what he could do to her father, Mary Ann let him sit on her porch in the evenings, and tried to pretend she didn't know what he'd come for.

That went on for three months, with Mary Ann crying herself quietly to sleep every night; and after a while there was even some lowdown gossip that she was going to accept Jonas Hackett for his money, and because of what he might do, and because his house was the finest house in the county, in the prettiest place.

(Grandma broke off, and I thought to myself she was making it up, because Hackett's Hill was the ugliest place in the county, not the prettiest. Besides, searching around, I couldn't see any sign of where a house might have been, not even a small one. But her face looked as if she was telling the truth. It made me feel queer.)

Then (Grandma said), the *Queen of the East* came in from the sea with Middleton Martin aboard, and he took the stage straight for home, wanting to get back to Mary Ann as fast as he could. But first, not knowing a thing, and it being right on the way, he stopped off a minute or two to leave Jonas a present. Jonas shook hands with him just as if nothing had happened, and Middleton gave him a bundle tied up in canvas, which he'd brought all the way from Foochow.

"Open it up," Middleton said.

So Jonas took off the canvas, and there was a sort of a cage about two feet square. It was made of lacquered wood and bamboo, and pieces of fancy red cord laced around and crisscrossed inside, and there were bits of silk like bright little flags at the corners, with Oriental writings.

"What is it?" asked Jonas.

All the Tea in China

"A tea merchant had it," Middleton told him. "He'd got it from one of the caravan men, who'd brought it in from the mountains out behind China. It's a demon trap. Suppose you want to catch you a demon. You set it down by some track where they run, and by morning most likely you'll find a big fat one." He slapped Jonas' back, and roared with laughter. "Works every time. Doesn't even need bait. It's just what you need!"

"What do they do with the demon?" Jonas asked him, not laughing at all.

Middleton cocked a red eyebrow, but he saw that Jonas was serious, so he made out like he was. "If he's a water-demon," he said, "they burn him up right there in the cage, but if he's a fire-demon—you can tell by the smell—then they chuck him into a well or a lake, cage and all."

Jonas frowned. Quickly he shoved the cage back behind him, as if to protect it. "*I* wouldn't do that," he declared.

Then Middleton told him good-bye, and went on up to Mary Ann's house. But that was just the first time he saw Jonas Hackett that day.

(Grandma snorted.) He found out soon enough. He was back inside half an hour, and Jonas, standing out on the porch, saw by the look on his face that he knew.

"*Well?*" he said.

Middleton spoke very softly. "Jonas, I didn't use to believe what folks said about you. I almost do now. What do you want with my Mary Ann?"

"I'm going to marry her," Jonas answered.

"Suppose she says no?"

"I can ruin her dad," Jonas said.

The shoulders of Middleton Martin's blue jacket went tight. "Suppose *I* say no, Jonas?"

"Berths are scarce, and you won't have yours," Jonas told him. "The *Queen* is *my* ship."

For a while they looked at each other without saying a word. Then Middleton said, "We've been friends, Jonas. We've been friends a long time. I guess we can still be. Just say you don't want her—that it's been a mistake. Give her up, Jonas."

All the blood left Jonas' lips. "Not for all the tea in China!" he snapped.

Middleton laughed in his face. "All right, have it your way. I've talked to Mary Ann. I've talked to her father. We're getting married next week. Wreck him—he'll be living with us. Take my berth—I've got a new one, a command of my own, bigger and faster." And with that he turned his back and walked off.

(Grandma shaded her eyes from the sun, and pointed east of the road.) The Thorpe place was just beyond Smathers'. Even now, you can hardly see it from here. Jonas spent some bad nights, I've been told, pacing the floor and saying never a word, all eaten inside because not two miles off were three people who'd told him where to head in. The truth was he'd gone off half-cocked. Middleton and Mary Ann and her pa knew the worst he could do, and they just didn't care. He kept thinking of Mary Ann being Mrs. Middleton Martin, and how folks in the valley would laugh in his face; and the closer they got to the wedding, the worse he became. Those who saw him said his hands were clinching and clenching harder than ever, and he walked with his teeth skinned back like a wolf's. Then, just two nights before the wedding was set to take place, he got his idea.

All the Tea in China

He was sitting in the dark in his parlor, thinking what he'd like to do to Middleton Martin, and racking his brains for some new dirty trick, when all of a sudden he stretched out his hand—and there was the demon-trap, which he'd completely forgotten. As soon as he touched it, the idea came into his head.

Jonas knew that Orientals know a lot of things better not known, and he figured that if they took the time to build demon-traps, those traps would most likely catch demons. Also, he knew there'd been demons and devils aplenty in Massachusetts back in the old Salem days, and that Satan himself still had business in Boston, because he'd been mixed up in it often enough. And he reasoned that if a little trap'd catch little devils, why it'd only take a great big one to catch the biggest of all.

Showing his teeth in the moonlight, Jonas walked out in the night to the Post Road, which ran right past his gate, and he looked up and down. In those days, it was straight as an arrow all the way down the valley, and he guessed that it was the track the Devil would use when he went up to Boston. Right away, he made up his mind that he'd catch him—but he wasn't intending to waste him by chucking him, sizzling and sputtering, into the ocean—not Jonas! He was going to keep him right there in the cage till he fixed it so he could get Mary Ann.

Jonas looked at the moon, and laughed without making a sound, and he went back in the house, and woke up his two foreign servants, a man and a woman, and sent them off into town to buy stuff—lumber and silk, and red-colored paint, and cord and bamboo. Later that day, old Lem Smathers saw him hammering away in the yard like a madman, with the big trap darned near finished, but he wouldn't tell Lem anything. It was the servants that told it next day, after it happened, because right at the last they found out what he was up to and ran off and quit him. The rest folks just figured out.

Night came, dark and angry, with storm clouds drowning the stars and hiding the moon except once in a while for just a few seconds. And Great-uncle Jonas hitched a team to his devil trap—for, making it strong, he'd built it too heavy to carry—and dragged it out, and set it up by the road right under his window. Then he went back in to stay up and watch, leaving the window propped open in spite of the weather so he could hear if anything happened. It stormed and it rained, and the wind blew and blew, and several times he had to go take a look, just in case, and he got soaked to the skin. But he didn't think about that. Then, toward three o'clock, the sky started to clear, and gales up aloft tore the black clouds to shreds—and all of a sudden, down by the trap, Jonas heard a stumbling and stamping, and a roaring and ranting like he'd never heard in his life.

Jonas knew that the worst thing you could do, going into a deal, was to seem to be anxious, so he walked down as slow as he could, his hands in his pockets. Sure enough, there was his trap, with its little silk flags fluttering their Oriental letters in the cold breeze. And sure enough, in it, all tangled up in the strings, was the Devil.

He didn't have hoofs or a tail, or anything like it. He was six-foot tall, dark and handsome. He wore a big beaver hat, and a greatcoat, and flowers all over his vest, and a gold watch and chain. When he saw Jonas Hackett, he quit his struggling and swearing, and tried to pretend not to be mad, and actually smiled.

All the Tea in China

"Good mawnin', suh," he said, bowing. "Mah name is Legree. Ah'm a tobacco auctioneer from No'th Carolina, headin' for Boston. Ah seem to have blundered into this heah Yankee contraption."

Jonas didn't bow back. "That's right," he agreed, "sure seems like you have. But you're no auctioneer, no more'n I am."

The Devil shrugged just a little, and fixed up his smile. "Ah see, suh," he said, "that Ah'm dealin' with a true judge of man's nature. Ah was lyin', suh, Ah admit it. But Ah was only tryin' to spare the Abolitionist sentiments heahabouts. Truth is, Ah'm a slave-dealer from way down in Memphis. And now, suh, Ah'll oblige you to set me free from this gadget—"

"You're a slave-dealer, right enough," Jonas answered, "but not like you meant it. Down South, you'd show up as a Yankee. I know you, Satan."

At that, the Devil couldn't help letting a wisp of steam, smoke, and flame leak out of his nostrils, and he quickly lit a cheroot trying to cover it up. Then he smiled again, a smile that would've scared most any man clean out of his skin. "You'd best open the door of this thing," he suggested, "before I break it down and come get you."

Jonas just shook his head. "If you could've, I guess you'd have got me already," he said coldly.

Well, the Devil couldn't control himself any longer, and the show he put on made all the cussing and roaring he'd gone in for before seem like nothing at all. He described the things that would happen to Jonas if he ever got out. He spouted out cinders and sparks, and smoke poured from him, and red flames; and the sulphur and brimstone smelled up the valley for days. He even took his true natural shape a few times.

But Jonas hung on, and didn't heed him at all, because he knew he could force him into a deal. And, watching real close, after almost an hour he saw him beginning to tire.

Finally, the Devil worked himself up to a real fever pitch. He grabbed the bars of the cage, and shook them till all the ground quaked, and in a voice like thunder and lightning he bawled, "OPEN THE DOOR!"

And Jonas knew at once that the Devil was just about done. He looked him right in the eye. "I wouldn't do *that*," he said firmly. "Not for all the tea in China. No siree bob."

There was a great dreadful hush, as if everything over the world had just stopped. Slowly, the Devil eased up. He lit another cheroot. He twirled his mustache. "Wouldn't you?" he said with a smile. *"Wouldn't you, Jonas?"*

Then and there, Jonas forgot all about Mary Ann, and what all the neighbors would say, and Middleton Martin. All he could think of was how much money there would be in that tea. "We-ell," he said to the Devil, *"maybe* I would."

"That's fine," said the Devil. "It's a deal!"

Jonas backed away from the door. He knew that the Devil had to keep that sort of a bargain. "Hold on a minute. That tea'll have to be packed in tea chests and bales, and set down right here."

"You're a hard man," the Devil declared, "but you've got me. That's the way it'll be."

"Shake," said Great-uncle Jonas; and they shook.

And then he opened the door....

All the Tea in China

Grandma eyed me very severely. "That was how Jonas Hackett came to his end," she said after a minute. "Let it be a lesson to you, boy. Don't you *ever* forget it!"

"Did—did he get all that tea from the Devil?" I gasped.

"Every last bit. There was one peal of thunder, and a flash from one end of the sky to the other, and, sure enough, there it was."

She paused. With a heel, she kicked at the thin inch of topsoil covering up Hackett's Hill. Under it was a thick, dark brown leaf-mold, and some rotten wood like the corner of a broken old chest; and the smell of tannin came up as strong as could be.

We looked at the Hill, more than 200 feet high and 1,000 feet long, sitting squarely on top of where Jonas' place used to be.

"All the tea in China," Grandma said. "Yes siree bob. There was a lot of it, too."